A SWEETWATER CANYON HOLIDAY TRIO

MAGGIE LYNCH

Windtree
Press

Windtree Press

http://windtreepress.com

Publisher's Note: This is a work of fiction. Names, characters, places, and incidents are a product of the author's imagination. Locales and public names are sometimes used for atmospheric purposes. Any resemblance to actual people, living or dead, or to businesses, companies, events, institutions, or locales is completely coincidental.

Cover Design by Christy Keerins

A Sweetwater Canyon Holiday Trio / Maggie Lynch. -- 1st ed.

ISBN 978-1-947983-19-9 ebook

ISBN 978-1-947983-61-8 print book

❁ Created with Vellum

PREFACE

This collection of three holiday stories written at different times during my writing of the first three novels in the Sweetwater Canyon Series, but are collected here as a holiday trio. **Hogmanay Stranger** was written after Book 2, **Healing Notes**. Thanks for Love was written after the third book, **Heart Strings**, in the Sweetwater Canyon series. Christmas Courage was written just before Christmas 2017 as a give-away to my fans.

Each of these stories stand on their own. However, if you are curious about what has happened before with these characters, please do check out the rest of the series. You will want to follow each of the characters through their own journey to manage a career, a family, and love.

In fact, you can get the first novel for free by signing up to my email list. Click the picture to go directly to the sign up page. Or go to my website and you will see the signup on the front page. https://maggielynch.com

Balancing a career and a relationship is never easy, and it's even harder when you are on the road and everyone wants a piece of you.

As a music major who sacrificed everything to become master of the upright bass, the last thing Michele Scott thought she'd be doing is touring with an Americana and Bluegrass band. But to tell the truth, she loves it.

Not so much David Blackstone. Even though he's irresistible, the thought of balancing her career, life on the road, and a long-distance relationship isn't for her. Her music gives her life, yet her heart yearns for something more. A girl just can't have it all… or can she? Trusting David is a risk that may give her everything she wants or it will close her heart forever.

GET YOUR FREE COPY NOW!

MAGGIE LYNCH

A
Sweetwater
Canyon
Novella

Thanks for Love

Windtree Press

http://windtreepress.com

Cover Design by Christy Keerins

Thanks for Love / Maggie Lynch. -- 1st ed.

ISBN 978-19436016-4-6 ebook

ISBN 978-19449737-8-0 print book

❀ Created with Vellum

This is for Christy Carlyle, my friend, fellow author, and walking partner. It is our walks that help to keep me healthy, and our friendship that keeps me sane. We discuss our characters, our plots, our writing careers, and share what's going on in our day-to-day lives.

Dear Readers,

Several months after I completed **_Heart Strings_**, I realized that there was much more I wanted to explore regarding all that happened between the time Tom rescued Sarah from Amanda's insanity and the ending of that book. At the time, I wasn't prepared to take that journey with Sarah. I was wrung out with the emotional journey I'd presented. However, after some time away I knew I had to tackle that story before I could move onto Theresa's story in Two Voices.

At first, I thought this story could be told fairly quickly in a novelette about the size of The Hogmanay Stranger. But the more I wrote, the more I realized that the emotional journey of Sarah, Tom and the children was much more complex than a shorter story could hold. It needed the extra time to unfold and to ensure no matter what challenges came in the future, they could still maintain their happily-ever-after ending.

I chose a Thanksgiving wedding because it aptly reflected Sarah's faith and gave me the chance to revisit the Thanksgiving of my childhood and how important those extended family and friend dinners were and still are to me today.

It was those Thanksgiving dinners that were a foundational part of forming my personal beliefs in families of all types and the permanence of love and faith—no matter how one's faith may be questioned or changed. For us, Thanksgiving was never commercialized and not in any way linked to Christmas. I've never been shopping on Black Friday, for example. Friday after Thanksgiving was still extended family time.

Family included siblings, aunts, uncles, cousins, foster children, grandparents, and a variety of combinations of "significant others." We would come from miles away to gather in one spot and give thanks together.

As children in our teens and early twenties, many of us brought a friend who had no family to share thanksgiving or were part of a family where the home was often not safe during the holidays. Thanksgiving also presented the first introduction of a significant romantic relationship in someone's life—girlfriend, boyfriend, or partner.

When my husband and I became serious, Thanksgiving was a "test" of our relationship. It was a kind of values statement of what family means and that he had to be an active part of this crazy, diverse family to understand me and support me throughout a marriage.

As a child, before saying grace, we were each required to mention at least one thing we were thankful for. At some of the larger gatherings (75+ people) this could take a while, but it was a ritual that reminded us of the importance of gratitude and to focus our mind before the prayer.

When I look back at this time, it is still miraculous to me. I realize how really blessed I've been with so much love and support throughout my life. Today, I still travel to celebrate Thanksgiving with my mother and those siblings, cousins, aunts and uncles, extended family and friends who are within a two to three hour drive. The numbers are much smaller as we've grown older and spread around the country. My grand nephews and nieces and cousins still occasionally bring friends who have nowhere to go. It is still a time to introduce a serious boyfriend, girlfriend, or partner. We still talk about what we are thankful for and we still have grace before eating. I am truly blessed.

I wish you an amazing Thanksgiving celebration wherever you find it. If you are able, consider inviting at least one other person who has nowhere to go or no family to share a meal. It will bless you at least as much as it also blesses them.

Maggie Lynch

Tom leaned over Sarah's hospital bed and brushed a light kiss across her bald head. She stirred but did not wake. Though she'd been alert when he'd finally found her at Amanda's cabin, the surgery, pain medication, and the need to sleep meant she only woke a few times a day and then only for a few moments. The untreated stab and whip wounds had become infected, causing sepsis.

It was the third morning they'd shared in the hospital. He hadn't left since he'd rode in the ambulance with her after enduring Amanda's insanity. He'd never forgive himself for all he'd done to bring Amanda into their life, both eight years ago and now.

Sarah's eyes fluttered open. She tried to move but groaned. "I feel like I've been run over by a semi." Her gravelly voice was barely a whisper as she struggled to speak.

"You may as well have been. Your body has been through a lot. It will take a while to get back to your energetic self." He paused and squeezed her hand. "Take it slow. You don't have to talk.

She groaned again and barely whispered, "What happened with Amanda?"

Tom clamped his jaw with the memory of everything Sarah had been through—the beatings, the knife cuts, the angry shaving of her head, the broken ribs—all because Amanda wanted Tom for herself, no matter what Tom wanted.

"She's in jail," he answered between his teeth. "And she's going to stay there a very long time."

"She was so raging, so hurt. I...actually felt sorry for her. Sarah said. "I prayed for her the entire time I was at that cabin."

"And how did that work out for you?" He bit his tongue at the harshness of his words. He didn't want to be angry with Sarah. He was still angry with himself and how his actions eight years ago had put all of this in play. Tom had no prayers for Amanda. In fact, if he had it in his power to send her straight to hell he wouldn't hesitate for even a moment.

"You sound angry," Sarah said.

"Damn right I'm angry. She had no right to think I'd be with her. She had no right to kidnap you and take her twisted feelings of revenge out on you. You could have died. If she needed revenge she should have kidnapped me.

Sarah put her hand over his closed fist. "It's not your fault."

"It is. If I'd never dated her...if I'd never been a scared teenager and left you...I must have done something to make her believe we would stay together."

"That was eight years ago, Tom. You can't be held accountable for something you did as a teenager. She got married. She had children. There was nothing that would make you think she would do this."

He ran his hand through his hair and shook his head. "There were signs. She kept coming on to me and I didn't take it seriously. I am accountable. I regretted dating her eight years ago, and I still regret it now."

"Obviously, she needs help. Killing her own husband ...with her children in the house?" Sarah closed her eyes and Tom saw tears trickling down her cheek.

He breathed deeply to calm himself. His anger was not helping Sarah heal. "I'm sorry," he said as he stroked her cheek with a finger. "I didn't mean to get worked up."

Sarah sighed and turned her head toward him. "Something is

definitely wrong with her. Something snapped." She paused and swallowed before continuing. "She was mean in high school but she was never out of control like this," Sarah said, her voice a little stronger. "That's why she needs my prayers. You have to let go, Tom. Don't let what she did eat you up inside. If you do, she'll come between us again, and I don't think I could survive losing you this time."

He shook his head with wonder. Sarah should be the one seeking revenge. He'd never known a woman like her—someone who was already on the road to forgiving Amanda, even after all she'd been through.

"What does that head shake mean?" she asked. "That you won't let go?"

"No, the revenge is that she will be in prison a very long time." He looked toward the corner of the room and his chest tightened. He fought to control his anger. "As for letting go…I can't. I'm no saint. Never have been and never will be."

"I'm not either," Sarah insisted.

He looked back and quirked a brow upward.

"I'm not—not even close. It's just that I've learned, through my own mistakes, that hating takes a lot more energy than I'm willing to give it." She paused and closed her eyes.

He waited, but it was as if this short conversation took all of her energy. She fell asleep again.

Tom leaned in and brushed her lips again. "Sweet dreams, love." He sighed and slipped back in his chair, his eyes closing for just a few minutes.

"How are Grady and Connor?" she asked as he began to nod off.

He smiled and moved back toward the bed, clasping her hand. "They're doing fine at the Rodgers' farm. I've called them every day to talk to them. They have a lot of questions about why you are in the hospital and if they can come see you."

Her forehead wrinkled. He wasn't sure if it was in concentration or in pain. "What have you told them so far?"

Tom's breath caught. He'd struggled with that question himself. He hadn't told them much, just enough to help them not worry. He hoped.

He drew his fingers up her arm to her throat, lightly caressing the bottom of her throat to her shoulder, alternating between the back of his hand and his fingertips. His fingers skimmed over the healing whip wounds along her clavicle. He wanted to kiss each one and have it heal as easily as a child's scraped knee.

"Tom?"

He swallowed hard, concentrating not to let any anger into his voice. "I told them we found their mommy, but that she is very sick and needed lots of help and they wouldn't see her for a very long time."

An audible breath escaped her lips. "That's good." She groaned as she shifted her weight a little to her side, so she could look directly at him. "And what have you told them about me?"

His caresses moved to her cheek; the cheek that was still black and blue from the punches she'd endured. "I told them you were hurt and had to go to the hospital and that you would be here at least a week. I told them that, when you are feeling better, I'll bring you back to the farm and they could come back to live with us."

"I want to see them," Sarah pronounced.

He shook his head. She seemed so fragile. "I don't think that's a good idea. If Connor and Grady see you like this they are going to ask a lot of questions about what happened. What will you say?"

Sarah took in a deep breath and let it out slowly. "I don't know what yet, but I also know that children can make up a lot worse things in their head about what is going on. Their mother left them. Their father was murdered while they were in the house. I'm sure they're thinking that we will leave them too or die." She placed a palm over his wrist. "I just want them to know I'm here for them. I want them to know that we will go back to being a family as soon as possible. I want them to know they are loved and we think of them as our children too."

"I want that too, Sarah. But..."

"How to reassure them without telling them their mother did this to me," she finished his thought for him. She closed her eyes again. "Why does it have to be so hard? It's not fair for two little boys to be saddled with all this hurt."

"It's not fair for you to take it all on yourself, either." He traced circles across the back of her hand.

"I'm not. It's just that…"

"You want to put this all behind you and move forward."

She sighed and then slowly nodded. "Come up here." She patted the bed in front of her.

He chuckled. "I don't think there's room for both of us."

"There is." She grunted as she tried to maneuver toward the railing on the opposite side.

He stood. "Hold on. Don't hurt yourself even more by trying to move so much."

She pushed against the bed and locked her lips in concentration as she scooted another couple inches, then rested. "I have to move. They make me walk every day, you know." She grunted again and scooted herself one more time. When she'd backed up against the opposite railing, she patted the bed again. "Come on now. Make all this work worth my while."

He gingerly maneuvered his way onto his side and stretched out on the bed, inching his arm beneath her pillow. He stayed as close to the edge as possible so as not to put any pressure from his body on her.

"Closer," she said. "Don't make me have to move back toward you."

He scooted closer and Sarah angled her body and nestled her head into his neck. "Closer," she said again.

He snuggled in until they touched from chest to toes. He couldn't help but put an arm across her with a soft embrace. Then he angled his head above her and kissed her. At first it was soft and nurturing. But then she returned his kisses with a demand that surprised him.

He responded in kind, barely able to contain his own urgency. "I love you, Sarah Cosgrave."

"I know." She sighed again, and turned her cheek toward the bed.

Her eyes closed and almost immediately he heard the even breathing of sleep.

Tom didn't dare move. He watched her chest rise and fall with every breath. Three days ago he wasn't sure she would ever breathe on her own again. During surgery, they said she went into cardiac arrest from the entire trauma she'd suffered—from what Amanda did and from the surgery. Since then he'd spent every moment they let him at her bedside.

He wanted her back at home. He wanted them married. He wanted the four of them to be a family again…but not before she was ready and stronger. The farm was a long way from a trauma center; and more than anything else, he just wanted her whole and healthy again.

He'd find a way to bring Grady and Connor in tomorrow. Together they would find a way to tell them enough to be truthful, but not more than they could understand. He knew how easily a child could feel betrayed when they weren't told the truth and found out later. But he also knew how easily a child's sense of who they were was formed by memories of their parents.

It was a complicated path that Sarah requested. But she was right. Connor and Grady were now family and they all needed to find a way to heal together.

"Thank you, Lord, for holding Sarah," he whispered. He closed his eyes and a feeling of peace calmed him. His breathing slowed and soon sleep came too.

*S*arah sat on the edge of the hospital bed taking deep breaths before trying to change into pajamas. No way was she going to greet the boys in an ugly hospital gown that exposed her backside. She planned to go on a walk with them to prove she was doing well and assuage any concerns.

She took in a deep breath and then let it out as she lifted a foot into the royal blue pajama bottom. A pain immediately shot to her groin. The whip cuts on her thighs had been especially deep there and infected. There were several layers of stitching. As the wounds healed they also tightened. Right now it felt as if she was pulling all those stitches apart, one by one, as she raised and lowered her leg.

She took another deep breath and then lifted the other leg. "Woo!" A breath rushed out at the end. That leg was a little easier. Clasping her fingers around the edge of the v-necked tee shirt, she pulled it into her lap. The white and pink stars on the blue background made her smile. She could get the boys talking about star constellations with this. She easily slid the oversized top over her head and past her bandaged ribs.

Wobbling as she stood, Sarah grasped the walker next to the bed and slowly stood straight.

"Well, well. Look at you!" Theresa's smiling face peered around the corner of the door. "Okay if I come in?"

Sarah nodded. "Good timing. I need to decide what to do about my hair."

"What hair?" Theresa asked with a laugh. "Just tell the boys you decided to leave boring Sweetwater Canyon and join a raucous punk band."

Sarah rolled her eyes. "Yeah, sure. They'll believe that." She pushed the walker toward the bathroom. "Need to look in the mirror and see how bad it is, so I can create a reasonable story for the boys."

She opened the door and the light automatically came on. She gasped. "I feel like a bald Bride of Frankenstein." She turned her head from side to side. "It seems to look worse now than it did when they first unwrapped the bandage from my head."

Theresa put an arm around Sarah's waist. "You were drugged then, sweetie. Believe me, it's better. Not as red."

Sarah's shoulders drooped. "I shouldn't have insisted that Tom bring them here. All I'll do is scare them."

Theresa looked in the mirror and then turned to look Sarah in the eyes. "We will *not* let that happen. I brought some help." She scooted toward the door to the room and yelled into the hall, "Come on in."

In the mirror reflection, Sarah saw Kat and Michele march past with several bulging shopping bags. Michele was first into the bathroom and stepped to Sarah's side, gingerly hugging her. Then Kat appeared as well.

"Where? What?" Sarah sputtered.

"Tom called to tell us he was bringing the boys by. We knew you would feel pretty self-conscious, so we brought the makeover team. So, how about you come back to the bed and sit up and we'll all decide how you want to look."

Kat peeked from behind Michele. "It's not as bad as you think."

Sarah rolled her eyes.

"Okay, it is as bad as you think, but wait till you see what we brought."

Sarah heard a rustle in the room, but couldn't see anything.

"Stop the chit-chat and get in here." Rachel's lilting brogue caught Sarah's attention. "We don't have a lot of time. To get you even close to being as good looking as me, we need to start now."

Sarah smiled and scooted her walker back into the room. She gasped at the assortment of items spread across the foot of the bed—multiple scarves with different colors and patterns, hats from subdued to outrageous, and a variety of clothing.

Rachel reached into one more bag and pulled out two wigs, both close to Sarah's original golden-brown hair color. "Do you want the cute short page boy or the long sexy Lady Godiva?"

Sarah chuckled as a grateful tear escaped. "You guys are the best." She wobbled a bit as she pushed toward the bed.

Theresa stepped in to steady her with a strong arm. "Let's get you settled. This makeover stuff is exhausting."

Kat quickly took the walker and moved it out of the way as Theresa helped lift Sarah's legs back onto the bed.

"Exhausting for us," Rachel joked. "You're just going to sit there and be waited on like a queen."

Sarah laughed again. Rachel always helped her not take life too seriously. Who would have known they would really become friends when they were so different.

"How far up do you want to sit?" Theresa asked, as she pressed the button to raise the head of the bed.

"Stop," Sarah said when she'd reached a comfortable angle. "A little up on the knees too, please."

When Sarah finally settled, Rachel minced over with the wigs. "What's your choice? Return to your long locks or a whole new look?"

Sarah looked from one to the other. Neither felt right. Though her hair had been practically to her waist before Amanda shaved it all off, she didn't want to return to the past.

"I think no wig," she finally said. "I don't want to scare the boys, but I don't want to be something I'm not either. It's going to take a long time to get my hair past the pixie stage."

"Good choice," Kat said. "Personally, I always thought a colorful scarf was the best way to go. You know kind of drape it across your head and then around your neck. It's all the style right now."

Kat fingered several different colors at the foot of the bed. She held up a cobalt-blue scarf with a subtle white, cloud pattern and handed it to Sarah. "Feel this. It is soooooo soft you'll want to sleep with it."

Sarah caressed the fabric with her fingertips. "Oh yes. I see what you mean. It's like brushed cotton or flannel."

"No wait," Kat said, now holding up a pastel blue scarf with multiple ocean colors. "Now this one is soft, lightweight, and won't highlight any dark patches." She draped it across Sarah's head and then around her neck. She held up a mirror. "See? It covers that bruise on your cheek and the lighter color evens out your skin tones."

Rachel stepped forward with a bottle in one hand. With the other hand she moved the scarf off Sarah's head and loosened it from around her neck. "I think this is just the right color, but your skin still needs a little help." She tapped out a bit from the bottle onto a fingertip and blended it all over Sarah's face. "This toner will even your skin tone, and then I'll add a little blush to make you look not quite as pale."

"Not too much," Sarah said. "You know I don't really wear much makeup."

Rachel brushed along her cheekbones with a light pink tone. "No worries. Just trying to put a little color back to make you look alive."

"And let's get rid of the astronomical pajama look," Theresa said. "You can be comfortable without looking bed-ridden or child-like."

"I thought it would be fun for the boys," Sarah countered.

"They want a mommy right now, not a playmate," Theresa said. She held up a navy drawstring pant. "These are comfy without being too tight." Then she put a long-sleeved, light blue mock-turtle top on top of the pants. "With the scarf Kat suggested, I think this outfit is comfy without being formal."

Sarah fingered the fabric of both the pants and the top. They were as soft as the scarf. "It's wonderful," she whispered, barely able to hold back from sobbing with gratefulness. Between all that had happened and her worry about the boys, she was overwhelmed and seemed to be more emotional than usual. "Thank you. Thanks for everything."

She looked at her band mates—her best friends. Everyone was silent for moment. They were gathered around her bed, not in pity but in complete support. She was so blessed.

"Mmm…hmmm." Rachel cleared her throat, breaking the silence. "These clothes aren't going to jump on you on their own. Do you want help or privacy?"

"Though I love these, and I'll keep them for another day, I'm sticking with what I have on," Sarah said. "I put in a lot of effort to get these on. The pants are plain but comfy. Yes the top has stars, but it makes me smile and I still think at least Grady will get a kick out of it. Besides the beautiful scarf covers most of it anyway."

Theresa lightly patted Sarah's thigh. "You would know the boys best."

Rachel added a few more touches of makeup. Kat primped with the scarf, and Michele brought her a soft, slippered shoe to wear when she was walking.

"Alright everyone, step away." Theresa put her hand on the curtain. "Let's go for the full reveal."

The other women giggled and moved away from the bed.

"Yes, Ma'am," Rachel saluted.

"Shall I play some intro music?" Kat asked. Though she had no instruments with her she made boom box sounds and Michele and Sarah started singing the Jeopardy tune. "Do do do do do do do."

Theresa stood near the bed. "Are you ready? Can I help you to stand?"

"If you can move my feet that will help a lot." Sarah said.

After some grunts and groans, Theresa slowly opened the curtain.

"Well?" Sarah asked. She stood beside the bed, one hand resting on the mattress to keep her balance. She was fully dressed head-to-toe, including a soft slipper shoe.

"Whoa!" Kat said. "You look hot. I mean for you."

"Kat!" Theresa scolded.

"I mean hotter than usual. Wait, I mean…you know…okay, I'll just shut up before my foot is totally buried in my mouth up to the knee."

Sarah could barely stay upright she was trying not to laugh at Kat's distress. "I know what you mean, Kat. I'm not someone who usually dresses to impress. I'm happiest in easy jeans, no makeup, and a bit messy."

"But you've always been hot underneath," Kat added, shifting from one foot to the other.

"Obviously," Rachel said. "She didn't get the bad boy of Broken Bow without something going for her." She walked over to Sarah and whispered in her ear. "I suggest you are not standing when Tom returns. Because he won't be able to stop himself from jumpin' your bones and that could be awkward with the boys around."

Sarah felt her cheeks warm. "Rachel, you know we've never…"

"Sure you haven't," she responded with an exaggerated wink.

Michele stepped up. "I think you look absolutely lovely. Modestly sophisticated casual. The boys will feel very reassured."

"Is that even a thing?" Sarah asked.

"Um, no," Rachel pronounced. "But it is an apt description of how you look and it fits you."

Sarah backed up to the bed and plopped on the edge. "I appreciate everything you all have done. Thank you! Now I don't have to worry about scaring the boys."

Theresa plumped the pillows. "You look beat. Can I help you get your feet back into the bed?"

Sarah nodded. She was really tired. Who knew that getting dressed could be so exhausting? "I'd like to get a little sleep before Tom gets back."

"Of course," they all echoed.

Kat folded the scarves they'd brought and opened one of the drawers in the wardrobe along the back wall. "I'm putting these in here, just so you have a choice another day."

Rachel pulled together the makeup kit and stored it in the bathroom. Then each of her band mates came up and gave her a hug, along with words about getting well and calling if she needed something.

She nodded and thanked them. "How long are ya'll staying in Oklahoma?"

"At least six weeks," Theresa said. "Michele and David set up some gigs for us and we wanted to be sure we could stick around to see you safe back at the farm."

"And I can help babysit, if you need," Kat offered.

"And any one of us can help with some basic chores, grocery shopping, whatever you need while you're recovering."

"Noel and Claire are flying in this weekend," Rachel added. "Claire is going to do a duet with me as part of our Saturday gig. She also wanted to meet the boys. She remembers how confused she was when her parents had problems. I think she could be a great example for them."

All Sarah could do was nod. Her heart was filled with the generosity of her friends. It was hard to even imagine being back at the farm right now. But it really was where she wanted to be.

Sarah waved goodbye to her friends and settled back into the pillows. She closed her eyes, and counted her many blessings. "Thank you, Father, for my friends in Sweetwater Canyon. And for Tom's abiding love. Please be with me when Grady and Connor come to visit today. Help me to say the right things. Help me to be realistic with them, as well as confident. Help us all to embrace each other and to be steadfast as we grow into the new family we will make together."

CHAPTER 3

$\mathcal{T}$om had a firm hold on each of the boy's hands. Grady on his left and Connor on the right were practically pulling him through the hospital corridor to visit Sarah. Tom still wasn't one hundred percent convinced this was the right thing to do. But he'd learned that Sarah was strong-willed and she was usually right when it came to people's needs.

As they turned the corner toward Sarah's room, Tom stopped and pulled the boys to him. "Grady. Connor. I need to tell you something before we go in."

"What?" They both asked, barely able to stand still.

"We already know everything," Connor, the oldest, said. "We know she's sick, we know not to bounce on the bed and all that stuff. We remember."

"Yeah, we 'member," Grady echoed in his four-year-old voice. "Don't worry. We careful."

"Also, she may look a little funny," Tom said. "Like a little red or black and blue."

Connor's eyes opened wide. "Did she get in a fight? Did someone try to hurt her like Daddy? Did someone try to kill her?"

"No!" Grady said. "*No!* No one kill Miss Sarah. No!"

This was exactly why Tom had been afraid of telling the boys anything about Sarah's injuries. He'd handled this part badly.

"Grady?"

Tom looked up at the voice. There was Sarah, standing in the hall with her walker. A vision in blue. She was covered from head to toe, but she didn't look really hurt. None of her scars showed. How did she do it?

Grady and Connor pulled at him. "Miss Sarah. Miss Sarah," Connor yelled. "Are you okay, Miss Sarah?"

Tom walked toward her, still hanging on tight to stop the boys from rushing her or pushing her over. When they reached her, Grady slipped out of his hand and wrapped his arms around Sarah's legs. "You're not killed, Miss Sarah. I'm glad you're not killed."

Sarah chuckled. "No, Grady, I'm not dead. I'm just recovering from some surgery."

Connor stood close to her but didn't hug her. He stubbed his toe in the ground. "You're not a zombie either."

"Come here, Connor." She wrapped her arm around his small shoulders. "I hope I don't look like a zombie. I tried very hard to look pretty today."

He hugged her tight. Tom stepped behind her for support and whispered in her ear. "You are a miracle, Sarah. How did you manage this?"

She smiled broadly. "The Sweetwater Canyon fairies can do magic." She tried to turn toward her room again, but the boys held tight to her legs.

"Boys?" She patted each of their heads. "I think I'm going to fall over because I've walked too much today. Can we go back in my room, and Mr. Tom can help me get back into bed? Then I can talk and answer all of your questions. Okay?"

They both nodded but didn't let go of her.

"She can't walk with you hugging her," Tom said. "Connor, you're the oldest. You get on that side." He pointed to the right. When Connor moved and took Sarah's right hand, Tom moved to her left and supported her with a firm arm. He felt her sag a little as she took on his support.

"What about me?" Grady asked. "I wanna help, too."

Sarah pointed to the door to her room. "If you would go in there and crawl up on the bed that would help. Make it good and warm so when I get in it I'm not cold. Okay?"

Grady raced away and Tom, Connor, and Sarah slowly moved back into the room. They found Grady snuggled up on the raised head part, and moving his legs back and forth.

"When my feet are cold in bed, this is what I do to make it warm," Grady said. "You try it, Miss Sarah. I think it's warm now."

"Thank you, Grady."

Tom helped Sarah to sit and then slowly raised her legs back onto the bed. He watched her grimace, but she didn't groan as she settled back in.

Sarah put an arm around Grady. "Thank you, it feels just right." She patted the side of the bed. "Connor, would you sit here please and keep the other side of the bed warm?"

Connor eagerly climbed up and she drew him into her side.

"Mr. Tom, would you pull the blanket over my feet and raise the foot of the bed a little?"

Tom complied, then pulled the chair he'd been sleeping in for three nights up to the bed's edge and gently laid a hand on her blanketed thigh. "We're all here now," he said. "One big happy family."

Sarah's eyes sparkled with unshed tears and he stood slightly to embrace her and the two boys. "All here," she echoed. "Thank you."

After only a few seconds, Grady pointed to Sarah's shirt. "Are those stars?"

"Yes," she said. Happy she'd stood up and decided to keep the shirt on. "Where do you think these stars are in the sky?"

"Right over our house?" Grady asked.

"That's exactly right, and when I get home we are going to sit outside and look at the stars and see what kinds of pictures they make. Do you know there is a picture of a warrior, and flying hourse, and a bow and arrow, and many things in the sky?

Grady's eyes widened. "Really? You aren't making this up."

"I know. I know." Connor said. "In school it's called consta... consta...lations."

"That's right," Sarah squeezed him against her side a little more. "Constellations."

Connor shifted a bit away from her. "Miss Sarah, can I ask you something?"

"Of course," she said.

"How come you have to be in the hospital? What happened to you?"

Tom braced himself for what she might say.

"Well, I kind of got caught up in a situation I couldn't control. And things happened that made me hurt. I got some cuts on parts of my body, like when you get rope burns on the tire swing but worse. So, I had to come to the hospital and get all fixed up."

Connor cocked his head to one side. "I don't see any cuts."

"I covered them up pretty good," she said. "But the worst part is I had to have all my hair shaved off."

"Really?" Grady asked. "Does that mean you have cancer?"

"No. I don't have cancer," Sarah replied. "It will start growing back really soon."

Connor swallowed. "Can we see or will it hurt too much."

"I can show you, if you don't think it will scare you."

"I'm brave," Connor said. "I can handle it, but if it's really bad I'm not sure about Grady."

Grady looked up at Sarah. "I'm brave too!"

"Okay. I'm going to take off my scarf. Are you ready?"

Both boys nodded, but their eyes grew wide as they watched her every movement.

Sarah slowly pushed back the scarf from the top of her head. "Do you see the redness there?"

"I see it," Connor looked at her. "Does it hurt real bad?"

"No, it's getting all better," she said.

"I wanna see more," Grady reached toward the scarf himself.

Tom reached out and stayed Grady's hand. "We have to be gentle. If we accidentally scratch her it might hurt."

Sarah pushed the scarf back until her scraped, bald head showed on its own. The two boys just stared.

"Mr. Tom," Grady said. "Please kiss it and make it better. Miss Sarah did that for me once and it really helped. But she can't kiss herself."

Sarah smiled and looked up at Tom. "That's a good idea, Grady. Mr. Tom, will you kiss it and make it better?"

Tom stood and leaned over. First he kissed her forehead. Then he kissed her on top of her head. "Are you feeling better?" he asked.

"Yes, I am," Sarah answered.

"Do it some more," Grady demanded. "It's a really big ouch." He pointed to the side of her head. "Kiss it there." Tom obeyed. Then Grady pointed to the other side. "Kiss it there." Again Tom obeyed.

Then Grady stood up and looked at everything. "I don't know if you have enough kisses, Mr. Tom. This is a lot."

Sarah burst out with laughter. "I think Mr. Tom has enough kisses, but I'm already feeling better so he can stop now."

Connor stared at her, his head down and his lips in a pout like he was about to cry.

She squeezed him toward her and nuzzled the top of his head. "I'm thinking I could get a part in a monster movie, what do you think?"

"I don't know."

"A zombie," Grady shouted and then laughed. "You could be a zombie and walk around like this." He held his arms in front of him and let his tongue hang to one side.

Tom couldn't help but chuckle.

"No, " Connor looked up and clenched his jaw. "Miss Sarah is too pretty for a zombie."

"Well, thank you, Connor," Sarah touched her head to his.

Connor's mouth again turned to a pout and his lips trembled slightly.

"Hmmm…it seems to me like you have some more questions. Is that right?"

"I don't know." Connor stared at the end of the bed.

"You don't know what?" Sarah asked.

"I don't know how this could happen. Who did this to you? Was it the bad man who killed my Daddy? Did he find you and hurt you?"

Tom stared at her and shook his head.

Sarah pulled Connor back into her side. "It was a person who really needed help, but didn't know how to ask for it. And I was there. Do you know how sometimes you get really mad and you really want to hit something?"

Connor nodded.

"And if you do hit somebody, you feel really bad and can't hardly remember what you were so mad about?"

"That happened once when I was little," Connor said. "I was really mad at Grady because he took one of my toys and I hit him. And he started crying. And then I felt really bad. I was scared, because I didn't want to hurt Grady, I just wanted my toy."

"That's kind of what happened to me," Sarah said. "A person got really mad at me because they couldn't get what they wanted."

"Is...that person going to get mad at me and Grady? Is she__I mean, could that person hurt us too? Connor asked.

"No," Tom said. "That person is in jail and will be there for a very long time."

Connor let out a breath. "Good." Then he relaxed against Sarah again. A few minutes later he heard Grady's little snores against Sarah's other side.

"Mr. Tom?" Connor whispered. "Are you and Miss Sarah going to be our mommy and daddy now? I don't want to go back to school without a mommy and daddy," he said. "I don't think our mommy really wants us anyway."

Tom looked at Sarah again. All he could think about was all the complications. How did she do it? How did she keep moving ahead in faith when everything around her was a storm?

"You know how much we love both of you, right?" Sarah said. "You know we will all be living on the farm again, just like a family. Even if we aren't officially your mommy and daddy, it doesn't change how much we love you."

Connor nodded.

"We have special permission to be your guardians," Tom continued for her. "Do you know what guardian means?"

"Yes, you explained that before. It means you take care of us." Connor sighed. "Okay. I guess that's okay…but…"

Tom waited for what followed but nothing more came out. "But what? What's really wrong, Connor?"

"But, I don't want to call you Mr. Tom and Miss Sarah anymore." Connor said.

"What do you want to call us?" Sarah asked.

"I can't tell you because I don't think you want me to say it. Also, I don't know how to explain it right."

"We can take our time," Tom said. "You try to explain it and we will see if we can help."

Connor crawled off the bed and stood next to Tom. He opened his mouth and then closed it again. "It's too hard."

"No matter what you say, we love you," Sarah said. "There is nothing you can say that will make us stop loving you. We will always be here for you, Connor."

He paced back and forth near the bed, his lower lip quivering. "If I …" He shook his head. "I can't say it." He paced some more. "I want…" Tom saw his eyes water and Connor swallowed several times. He didn't know what to do. What was so scary for him to ask?

"Connor, come here," Sarah said. "Give me your hand."

Connor did what she asked and she squeezed his hand.

"Now, close your eyes. Remember when I told you that you can tell God anything?"

Connor nodded.

"I want you to keep your eyes closed and talk to God right now. You can talk out loud or you can talk to him in your mind. You choose. You tell him what is so hard to tell us. Even if you can't explain it, God will understand. Okay?"

Connor nodded again. Then he knelt beside the hospital bed.

"Dear God. Miss Sarah said I could talk to you. I want to believe you can hear me, but I'm not sure. I have a problem and I don't know how to talk to Mr. Tom and Miss Sarah about it." He let out a big breath.

"I know they love me, but they don't really want to be my mommy and daddy. But the problem is I really want Mr. Tom to my daddy now because I don't have a daddy. I know Miss Sarah says he's in heaven now but I don't hear him talking to me and I want a daddy who talks to me. And I love Mr. Tom and I think he could be my daddy who talks to me. But he doesn't want me to call him daddy, and I don't know what to do."

Connor started crying softly. "And I don't know if I love my mommy anymore. I think she hurt my Daddy, but I can't tell anyone because I don't know for sure. But that is what the sheriff thinks even though he didn't tell me. And no one wants to tell me the truth and I don't know what to do."

Connor buried his face into the side of the bed as he sobbed. "I'm only seven." He choked out the words. "I need a daddy and a mommy, but no one really wants me. God, please help me."

"Tom!" Sarah cried softly.

Tom gathered Connor into his arms and climbed onto the side of the bed so that both he and Sarah could hold him.

"God hears you, Connor, whenever you talk to him. I try to talk out my questions too. One of the things Miss Sarah and I have talked about is doing the right thing for you and your brother."

Connor lifted tear filled eyes to Tom. "Really? What did you talk about?"

"Sarah kissed him on the forehead. "We talked about how much we love you and Grady and how we want to take care of you in the best way possible."

"I'll never replace your Dad," Tom said. "He was a great man who loved you very much. But I would be happy to be your second dad, if you'll have me. And I'd be ecstatic if you call me Daddy. I want to be your daddy more than anything in the world."

Sarah patted Connor's back as she let her own tears flow along with his. "Father, thank you for listening to Connor. Thank you for bringing Connor and Grady into our lives. Help me to be the best mother for both of these boys. Lead us all in the way of light. Guide us through the darkness and the complications yet to come."

Then Sarah started whispering and Tom could no longer hear her prayer. All he knew is that he couldn't let down these boys. He looked to each of them with tears in their eyes as the clung to him and Sarah. His chest clenched at how they had struggled, all they'd been through. He drew in a shaky breath and wondered if he could be even half the father Henry was. He never thought he'd be a father so quickly or have an instant family. But he would make this work. He could never let these boys face their future alone or be adopted to someone they didn't know.

Sarah finished her silent prayer and squeezed his hand. "Amen."

He let out the trapped breath he'd held. With Sarah at his side he knew could face this challenge. Just a few months ago, he never thought Sarah would ever love him again. He didn't have her faith. He didn't know if he believed in her God. But he believed in love—the kind of love and perseverance Sarah had shown through all her trials.

If Sarah could love these boys and be willing to make this a family, he could too. Better than could, he *would* make this their family.

Tom shook his head in amazement at how quickly things had changed in the past month. With the boys now needing a mommy and a daddy, he and Sarah needed to get married as soon as possible and officially adopt them.

CHAPTER 4

$\mathcal{S}$arah waited in the car while Tom carried her things to the front porch. He'd packed her clothes into a suitcase and all the cards and gifts she'd collected from friends and neighbors while she'd been in the hospital in the past few weeks. She still held the beautiful bouquet of mums he'd brought to celebrate her homecoming.

She couldn't help but touch the top of her head to make sure the peach fuzz hair was growing back.

After three weeks in the hospital, she was more than ready to be home. She no longer needed the walker, and her hair had grown enough to cover all the scars. In another two to three months, she'd at least have that pixie cut look. In the meantime, she used the scarves her friends had given her. The nurses had teased she was starting a fashion trend. Now all the patients would want to wear headscarves all the time.

Her main priority now was to build her strength so she could be a good mother to Grady and Connor. She and Tom had settled on a Thanksgiving wedding, and that was only three months away.

Sarah rolled her shoulders in backward circles. Everything tensed whenever she started feeling overwhelmed. She concentrated on her breathing. Her gaze wandered about the property, comparing it to her memories.

She turned her head slightly toward the barn remembering where Tom had slept when she first returned to Broken Bow. He'd lived in that little one-room studio he'd built. Even with all that had gone on with her father's illness and death, some of her best memories were with Tom in that room.

Her gaze traveled to the small field where they'd planted vegetables to be harvested right now. It was brimming with row upon row of beets, cabbage, cauliflower, fennel, potatoes, rosemary, rue and even more things she'd forgotten they'd planted together.

Farthest from the porch was a small section of corn. The stalks were so tall now just waiting to be picked. She wondered when she would have the strength to harvest the crops. And whether she'd be strong enough before winter to help till the soil and prepare it for next springs crop.

Tom knocked on the window, stopping her from getting lost in her thoughts. "Doing okay?" he asked as he opened the car door.

"I'm not sure," she said. "There is so much that needs to get done."

Tom offered his hand to her through the door. She hesitated for a moment, wondering if she was up to the challenge of being a good mother and wife. But then she shook her head at the thought and put her hand in his. She pushed herself up as he gently pulled her to stand. After she got her balance she said, "Ready."

He offered his left arm for support. "One step at a time."

She nodded, forcing a smile on her face. One step at a time. One day at a time. That had been her mantra during physical therapy at the hospital. Now she had to think one week at a time. One month at a time. How would she ever be ready for a wedding in three months?

As she scuffled across the dirt, she hesitated for a moment. She suddenly had a hard time picturing herself back in the house with Tom and the boys. It wasn't that she didn't love them, she did. In fact, she loved them more than anything in her life right now. Even more than her Sweetwater Canyon sisters.

Sarah had always wanted a family, although she pictured having some time alone first with whoever her husband would be. She pictured maybe two or three years, maybe even five, of just getting to know each other before deciding where they wanted to live, what they wanted to do, how many children they would have. But now she was faced with an instant family of four. She hadn't even had a chance to think about if she wanted more children than the two boys. The future was all suddenly overwhelming.

"Do you need me to carry you?" Tom asked.

She shook her head and leaned only slightly on Tom's arm as she started walking again. Finally, they made it to the front porch. She stopped at the small step up to the porch. She wanted to do it herself. She'd practiced taking a step in the hospital so she'd know how to navigate when she got home.

"What can I do?" Tom asked.

"Just let me figure it out," she said, regretting the snippiness in her voice. She placed her left hand on top the porch rail and raised her foot to the stair. Her arm shook as she pushed hard against the rail to raise her body and haul her second foot up. Refusing to groan or show any sign of distress, she stood tall with both feet planted firmly on the porch.

She noticed Tom was positioned close behind her, ready to catch her if she fell. "Stop looking at my butt and get the front door," she quipped.

"And a fine butt it is," he said. "Are you sure you can't handle the door on your own so I can continue to enjoy the view."

Sarah laughed. "It's my turn, mister. Now get in front of me."

He took two large strides and opened the door, exaggerating each movement before bowing. "Your castle awaits, Miss. Dinner will be served at six o'clock sharp" He extended a hand to help her over the threshold. Once she was inside, he asked, "Would you prefer to take your meal in the dining room this evening or shall I order room service?"

She couldn't help but laugh and want to play along. "That depends. Do I have to dress for dinner?"

Tom quirked an eyebrow and opened his eyes wide. "If you wish to come naked to dinner I will not complain. However, I might suggest we schedule your dinner at a later time, after the boys are asleep."

She felt her cheeks warm with embarrassment. "No, no. You know that's not what I meant." She was not experienced with sexual innuendo, and yet Tom always brought it out in her and then she didn't know where to go from there.

"My apologies, miss. I thought perhaps you were in the dream-fulfillment business."

"Oh my goodness." She fluttered a hand and grasped at the doorjamb. "I don't know what to say. I …"

Tom stepped in front of her and folded his arms around her waist, providing full support of her standing. "You don't need to say anything." He lowered his mouth toward her lips, his eyes locked onto hers. She'd forgotten how his eyes glittered with streaks of gold through the brown.

She could feel every breath he took and her heart matched that rhythm. Just as the longing became unbearable, Tom lowered his mouth and slowly feathered kisses along her lower lip and then the upper, teasing her open. At first he kissed her gently, carefully, as if she might break.

But it wasn't gentleness she wanted, not after all she'd been through. She wanted to be lost in him. She wanted to be kissed like he'd never let her go. She wanted to seal their hearts to each other. She knotted her fist in his shirt and pulled him harder against her, pressing her own lips into his, opening her mouth to invite him in.

He groaned low in his throat. "Sarah." Then he placed an arm beneath her legs and gently lifted her up, getting her to nestle into his chest. He strode down the hall to her bedroom, and toed open the door.

Her mind became hazy as their tongues danced together and he followed her lips down to the bed. She was exhilarated, yet scared. She wasn't sure what she'd started and she knew she couldn't finish. "Tom, I…" she gasped between kisses.

He hovered over her, moving his lips to her neck. His lips next lightly brushed multiple kisses over her bald head, and then down to her earlobes and across her cheekbone. "I can't get enough of you, Sarah. I've been waiting so long."

Her heart raced, followed by her own breathing. She couldn't think straight. All she knew was that she never wanted this to stop. He wasn't turned off by her scars, her missing hair. He seemed to still find her attractive.

"I won't hurt you," he said before recapturing her mouth again with a combination of soft and hard pressure. Then he backed off and gently caressed her lower lip. "Tell me if I'm hurting you in any way."

She couldn't speak as he prodded her mouth open once more and in one movement stole her breath, just to give it back again when she needed to breathe to live. Now she understood why Michele and Rachel described great kisses as the sensation of melting into one another. Though no part of him touched her except his mouth, she felt his body heat so close that she could swear their bodies were one. She arched toward him, her lips closing over his tongue. She wanted to breathe him into her soul, to never let him go. "Closer," she whispered. "I want you closer."

When she was at the brink of her world exploding, and wondering if begging him to take her would relieve the pressure building up under her skin, his mouth slowly withdrew. He feathered butterfly kisses along her neck and across her tee shirt at the shoulder as he rolled to one side and draped his arm across her belly.

An explosive warmth spread from her chest down to her toes, and she immediately yearned for more but didn't have the strength to move or speak.

"Maybe we should move up the wedding," Tom said, his voice no more able to sustain air than hers.

"Mmm hmmm," was all she could manage to say.

Tom chuckled. "It can be even better than kissing."

Sarah moved her head from side to side in denial. "Dead," she said. If it was more than she'd just experienced, she was certain she would die from the explosion.

The bed rocked as Tom rolled off the other side. Immediately her body shivered with his absence.

He pulled an afghan from the end of the bed and draped it over her. Then he leaned over and brushed his lips against her forehead. "You get a little rest so you have energy for dinner later."

She reached for his face with one hand. "Thank you."

He pressed his palm over her hand at his face. "For what?"

"For loving me."

He grinned and pressed her hand back to her chest. "Forever. I will love you forever."

Sarah closed her eyes. Just as she was about to fall asleep she heard Tom whisper, "You saved me, Sarah Cosgrove. You saved *me*. Now it's my turn."

SARAH ROLLED over and looked at the alarm clock. 5:30 a.m. She barely remembered eating dinner last night. Even with the nap after Tom brought her home, she'd still been exhausted when she awoke for dinner. Tom had proven his cooking skills were more than adequate. He'd baked chicken thighs in a sweet vinaigrette dressing, steamed fresh broccoli florets with a little butter, and created a sumptuous garlic sweet potato side dish. She wasn't sure how much she'd eaten before starting to nod off at the table and apologizing for not being able to finish her portion. He'd laughed and carried her back to bed.

After a stop in the bathroom, Sarah gingerly took one step and then another down the hall, making her way to the living room. She didn't hear any sounds in the kitchen. She smiled. Tom wasn't up yet and she could take her time without him hovering over her.

She wrapped her robe tightly around her, picked up an afghan on the sofa and slowly made her way to the front door. She needed to sit outside. She needed to breathe fresh air, not that recycled hospital air. She wanted to watch the sunrise and bask in being home once more. She wanted to slowly get her soul back into being comfortable with the farm.

Her hand firm on the front door, she slowly pushed it open, hoping it wouldn't squeak. Just when she thought she'd made it, a loud squeak at the hinge startled her. She stood perfectly still, holding her breath and listening for Tom. No movement. Good she hadn't awakened him. She tentatively stepped over the threshold and onto the porch. Every step she took seemed to ring out. She didn't want to wake Tom. She wanted these moments to herself. She quickly decided not to chance closing the door again.

Sarah eyed the Adirondack chair closest to the door. The question was if she got into it, would she be able to get out of it? What the heck? She couldn't stand here for even a few minutes, never mind the hour or two she wanted to be outside. So what choice did she have?

She positioned herself on the edge and then slowly scooted her bottom into the crevice and leaned back. With some effort she lifted each leg to rest over the curved wooden footstool.

Yes, she could do this. She would work to get stronger each day and soon she'd be doing whatever was needed around the farm, just like she did before her father died. Satisfied with her efforts, she closed her eyes for a moment and smiled, breathing in the misty morning air.

TOM'S HEART skipped a beat when he woke and saw the front door open. No! Amanda was in prison. She couldn't have taken Sarah again. Swallowing his fear he strode toward the door and peered onto the porch. Sarah was asleep in the chair, an afghan across her lap and legs.

His lungs filled with air once again and he matched her every breath to slow down his pulse. Her serene countenance, coupled with the fluffy white robe, reminded him of angel pictures. It made him smile. If he believed in angels, he was certain she had some wings tucked into her back somewhere. He stepped forward to move a stray hair from her eyes but then stayed his hand. He hadn't seen her this peaceful in months. The last thing he wanted to do was disturb whatever sweet dreams made her so calm.

It made him question their plan to get the boys from the Rogers' farm today. He wondered if it was too soon, if bringing them home to live full time with them now would prove to be too much for her. He shook his head. She'd insisted she wanted them back the minute she arrived on the farm. It had taken every bit of convincing to have her wait until she had one night at home.

As if she'd heard his questions in her head, she stirred. "Tom, are the boys here?" she asked without opening her eyes.

He stepped onto the porch and brushed a kiss across her forehead. "Good morning, love. It's only seven o'clock. I suspect they are helping the Rogers with the milking right now. How are you feeling?"

"Mmmmm."

"When did you make your way to the porch?"

Her eyes fluttered open and she turned toward him, a big smile on her face. "Oh dark thirty?"

"Midnight? Surely..."

She giggled. "No. Somewhere between five and six I think. I wanted to see the sunrise. Did I miss it?"

"No big sunrise this morning, I'm afraid. Weather report says the mist won't burn off until ten or eleven."

"Hmmm."

He wasn't sure if that hmmm was acceptance, regret, or something else all together.

"Can I get you some coffee?"

She nodded and pulled the afghan farther toward her chest. "And something sweet to go with it."

"I'm right here," he said.

She laughed, just as he hoped. "Yes, but I'm not going to eat you for breakfast."

"Even if I sprinkle myself in sugar?" he asked.

She turned a shade of pink. "I'm not sure if that's a thing, or you're just teasing. But the answer is no either way."

"Oh, it's definitely a thing," he said, mostly to see her blush again. "But for now I'll do your bidding and bring you coffee and a cinnamon roll."

"Thanks...sweet thing," she said. "Maybe, when we're married..."

He laughed again as he headed to the kitchen. When they were married, he thought. He'd been waiting for that possibility for more than eight years. Happiness fizzed through him. He felt he might explode like a bottle of champagne.

AFTER A LEISURELY BREAKFAST together on the porch, Tom held Sarah's hand as they watched the sun burn off the fog. As if they were an old married couple, she followed him inside and insisted on doing the dishes.

"Are you sure?" he asked. "You've barely been home a day. I can take care of it."

Sarah leaned on the sink and took a moment to think of her response. She didn't want to be smothered in his caring…his worrying about her. She didn't know what to do with that. She wished he would just be Tom—not a parent and nursemaid and housekeeper all wrapped up in one person. With all those other people inside him it was hard to find the Tom she wanted to love: the best friend turned future lover.

"Is something wrong?" From behind her, Tom wrapped his arms around her middle. He nuzzled the back of her neck. "I'm so glad you're home." Her heart melted and she turned in his arms toward his kiss.

As her lips moved along with his she wanted to make it deeper, more meaningful. She loved kissing Tom. She loved having his arms around her. She loved knowing that her best friend was going to be her husband soon. If only they could stay in this moment, and not have her recovery hanging over their heads all the time.

He drew his lips to a close and held her head against his chest. "If you're ready, I'll go get the boys now. I know they're really anxious to get home for good." He gently turned her face upward and looked directly into her eyes. "You are ready, aren't you?"

She nodded and swallowed anything she might say. She wasn't really sure, but what was there to do about it? She just needed to jump in with both feet and have faith it was all going to work out.

He feathered one more kiss across her cheek, then turned and ambled toward the door. Waving goodbye as he stepped onto the porch, he turned and said, "Don't try to do anything else while I'm gone. Just rest. The boys and I can handle everything for the next couple weeks until you're fully recovered."

Once more her teeth clenched at his over-protectiveness. She tried for some type of smile but failed. Instead, she wiggled her fingers goodbye. It wasn't until she heard the truck rev and then tires chewing up the gravel drive that she could let go of her irritation.

I'm not going to be overwhelmed, she told herself. There's nothing I can't do if I put my mind to it. Determined, she walked down the hall at a more confident pace.

She decided to start in her bedroom. Tom had left her overnight case there. She was sure it wouldn't overtax her to unpack and put things away. It would help her get the feel of the place again, and then everything would be okay. Everything would start to feel normal again.

She rolled her suitcase toward the bed then bent to lift it on top. She grunted with the exertion and felt light-headed. "This is *not* that hard," she reassured herself. "I used to lift fifty-pound bales of hay and throw them on the back of the truck with ease, then unload them in the barn. This little suitcase is nothing."

Regaining her balance, she opened the top and lifted a small pile of her underthings and walked the few steps to the dresser. Then she returned for her T-shirts and pajamas, taking time to arrange everything for easy access.

She retrieved hangers from the closet and turned toward her pile of blouses and pants. A sudden unease washed over her. She sat on the edge of the bed shaking. She could hear her heart pounding with every breath she took. Slow down, she told herself. Deep breaths. One. Two. Three. Breathe in. Breathe out. What was wrong with her? Everything was going so well.

Maybe she had to accept a little rest. In the hospital her only exercise was walking the corridor very slowly and an occasional visit to the bathroom. Even though they had her walking up and down the halls, it was probably three hundred feet maximum. And that was at a very slow pace.

She took a deep breath and lifted her feet onto the bed. She positioned herself against the stacked pillows and concentrated on her breathing. It was better, but still too quick. She closed her eyes.

"Mommy, Mommy! Where are you, Mommy?"

She woke with a start, hearing tiny feet slapping against the floor. Grady rushed into the bedroom, climbed up on the bed and surrounded her with giggles interspersed with question after question. She couldn't keep up.

Connor stood quietly on the other side, looking at her with concern.

Tom stood at the door smiling. "No rest for the wicked," he said. "Or even for the good."

She took a few minutes to muss Grady's hair and listen to adventure stories of what had been happening on the Rogers' farm for the past couple days since she last saw them at the hospital.

"And what about you, Connor?" she asked.

"Uh, nothing new," he said.

"Are you sure? You're being kind of quiet there."

"Just thinking." Connor stepped toward her head. "I missed you. I thought maybe you were dead when I looked in here before. Then Grady came runnin' and jumped on the bed."

Sarah's heart broke for him. He was still very worried about anyone he loved dying again. She'd talk to Tom this evening about getting some grief counseling for Connor. He needed a safe place to unload everything and not be afraid of freaking out the adults.

She squeezed his hand. "Nope. Not dead. I'm afraid you are stuck with me for a very, very long time whether you like it or not."

She reached toward him to tickle his sides. "Unless you want me to put on a sheet and do ghostly hauntings every night until I tickle you to death."

"Yes!" Grady yelled. "Yes! We want ghosts. We want ghosts."

Connor smiled just a little.

"I'll bet in a couple of weeks, you'll wish I was sleeping more often," Sarah continued. She mussed Connor's hair just as she had Grady's. "By then I might even be ready to beat you in a contest of who can shuck corn the fastest."

"It's a bet," Connor said, his smile more genuine now.

Tom stepped from the doorway. "Why don't you guys go to your bedrooms and get unpacked? You have to get everything neatly placed in your bedroom, and make sure all your things are ready for school tomorrow."

"Do we have to?" Connor asked. "I think we should skip so we can take care of Mom."

"Oh no you don't." Sarah poked a finger into Connor. "You aren't going to use me as an excuse to miss your education."

"My school's only half day, so I don't have to do very much." Grady stood his hands on his hips, legs spread wide apart, as if he was in charge.

"All you have to do is write a note to the principal," Connor said. "It's easy. Lots of people do it."

"Not gonna happen," Tom said as he stuck out his thumb and pointed it over his shoulder toward the door. "Mommy needs to rest a little more. When you have your room straightened out, you can both come help me in the kitchen."

"Hey!" Grady jumped off the bed and danced around the room. "Do I get to cook? Do I? Do I?"

"You can help me put the sliced bread on a plate, and Connor can help by setting the table."

Connor looked at Sarah then back to Tom, and then back to Sarah again. He looked as if he was going to argue about skipping school. Or play them one against the other. "Okay," he drew out the agreement. "But just for a couple days. When Mom is all better she can set the table."

Sarah laughed. She'd forgotten how dramatic children could be even when they were agreeing to do something. "Thank you, boys. You're the best. I don't know what I would do without you."

Tom signaled for the boys to get on with it and they slowly marched out the door toward their bedrooms. "And keep it neat," he yelled down the hall.

When he heard a bedroom door open and the boys already fighting over who got which dresser, he turned toward Sarah. "Finally a little quiet." He ran the back of his hand down her arm. "Are you holding up? Now that you've seen the energetic boys back in their element? I can keep them out of here as long as you want."

"No, no. I'm fine. Just close the door and give me a little time to organize my thoughts. I'll see what I can do to help in the kitchen."

"That's not necessary. Let us take care of you for a little bit."

Sarah shook her head. "I'm not an invalid. I want to be of help. I want to fit back into the day-to-day living as a family. I want to prove to the boys that we are going to make it. I want us to be happy together."

Tom sat on the edge of the bed and entwined his hand with hers. "Sarah, we have the rest of our lives together. There's no need to feel like you have to cram it all into these next few days."

"I know." She looked down at their interlaced fingers and squeezed. "I just... I just want to be done with everything related to Amanda, the hospital, and all the bad memories. I want to start making new memories...right now. Today! I need new memories to replace the last few months." He leaned over and hugged her tight. "You understand?" she asked.

Tom nodded. "I'm here for you, in whatever way you want, in whatever way you need." His thumb slid along her cheek to remove the tears that had formed against her will. "It's okay to be sad. It's okay to be confused. I don't know how you're able to hang on so well. I don't think I could do it."

"You could," she said. "You're a great father. I can tell the boys love you. No matter what happens to me I'm sure they'll be great with you."

He sat up straight. "What are you saying?" He looked her in the eyes. She could almost hear the wheels in his head turning. "What do you mean by 'what happens to me'?"

"I don't know." A cold shiver ran over her entire body. She couldn't stop the shaking. "I…I've been thinking a lot about what happened and how you could have been killed if you didn't do what Amanda wanted."

"But that's not what happened." He looked into her eyes and she couldn't help but realize how much she would be giving up when she left. But it was the only way to keep everyone safe. "She's in prison, for the rest of her life. She can't hurt us anymore."

"I know. It's not just her. It's the world. What if something happened to me again? What if I never get strong enough to be a good wife…to be the kind of mother Connor and Grady need? What if I can't ever get over this?"

Tom gathered her into his arms. "Where is all of this coming from, Sarah?

She couldn't stop the tears now, the tears she hadn't yet shed as she tried to be strong, to move on, to be the one who could do everything she did before.

She clutched at his shirt and tried to speak without choking. "I'm just not the person I was before…before everything happened. I used to believe nothing horrible would happen to me because of my faith. I used to believe God watched over me and protected me. Now I know that isn't true. Bad things can happen to me, just like everyone else."

Tom rocked her slowly, holding her head against his chest. "Oh, God, Sarah. I don't know what to say. You've always been the one with unwavering faith."

She cried aloud. That was it. She now questioned her faith. She questioned everything she believed to be true. How could she be a wife and a mother and have no faith?

"I don't know why bad things happen to good people," Tom said quietly. "I suspect it is a question every pastor in every church has to answer many times. It is one that has stopped me from understanding the faith you've had."

"Not any more," she mumbled.

She could hear Tom taking slow, labored breaths. She felt bad for failing him. She realized she had held a subconscious belief that she could bring him to faith by her example. Now she had failed him and herself.

"Sarah, whatever my own lack of faith, I cannot hold God responsible for the evil in the world. One thing you taught me eight years ago and have reinforced it since your return is that we have to forgive the world for not being perfect and go on living anyway. If each of us does this, lives our values every day despite all the bad things that happen, it is perhaps the only way we can expect change. The only way we make a difference.

"You've made a difference in my life even as a good-for-nothing teenager. When I watched how you dealt with your father, despite your past, despite his choices, I know you made a difference in his life too.

"You made a difference already in Connor and Grady's life, just by being you…just by moving forward, putting one step in front of the other every day. You could have chosen to hate them or at least ignore them or be scared of them because of everything Amanda did. But instead you love them.

"Nothing bad happens for any good reason. But I've learned that we have the capability to give bad things meaning. We can impose our meaning on them in order to move forward. We have to choose to live our lives the best way we can and to find a way to turn suffering into something meaningful—something that can propel us toward the light, toward good."

Sara let go of Tom and slumped against the pillow. She closed her eyes and couldn't help but smile. "For not being a believer, you just delivered an interesting sermon."

Tom shook his head. "No sermon. I just…" He let out a big sigh. "Just know how much I love you. How much so many people love you. Love has power over evil. Think on that too."

She could barely keep her eyes open. It was as if someone had pushed a weight onto her chest. Though Tom had pushed it off again, she still couldn't quite breathe. Her chest still felt crushed, unable to re-inflate.

"I'm just tired," she finally said.

He leaned over and kissed her forehead, then brushed his mouth across each of her eyelids. When his kisses reached her lips she returned it with the urgency of someone who knew she was lost and wanted to her find her way back. When Tom ended the kiss she sucked in a breath and locked her jaw against the need to beg him to stay.

Tom stood and trailed a finger along her arm. "Once you get some sleep I'll call you when dinner is ready. You just need some rest."

She nodded and closed her eyes, hoping he would leave her to her thoughts.

He kissed her once again. "I love you. Don't forget that. I love you. We will work all this out."

She kept her eyes closed and finally she heard him walk out the door.

Heavenly Father, I do still believe in you. I just don't understand. And it frightens me. She prayed. *I've only been home a day and I'm questioning everything. Am I doing the right thing by staying in this family, even if I can't contribute? Though it would break my heart, I could leave and give Tom a chance to find a good, strong woman to help him raise these boys. Please, show me a sign. Help me do the right thing...even if it's hard.*

CHAPTER 5

They had made a ritual of rising early on Saturday and sharing breakfast on the front porch together, just as they'd done that first morning after she came home from the hospital. The boys usually slept in until nine and it was this time between seven and nine that they had pieced together with some quiet before the chaos of the day ensued.

By October, Sarah was feeling more herself. Her hair had grown in and it was a nice pixie style that covered her head. If people didn't know her past, they'd think that was her natural choice to always wear her hair short. The best part was she didn't have to worry about styling, and after a shampoo it dried really quickly.

She could easily walk a mile now and was feeling more content in her role as a mother to two boys.

"What would you think about a small corn maze this year?" Tom asked. "I've sketched out a design that isn't too hard for the younger ones, but also not too easy for kids up to about ten." He sat on the wooden ottoman and faced Sarah, putting his large two-by-two-foot sketch on her lap so he had to read it upside down.

"I have two entrances and two exits." He traced the maze on the paper in a vertical motion, moving down her thigh, and then just when she thought she couldn't take it any more he reversed course and moved back toward her ankle. "This one is the more complex path for the older kids and adults. It has a lot more twists and turns, and dead ends. They could easily spend a couple hours getting lost."

Sarah sucked in a breath as she felt the pressure of his finger through the paper and onto her pajamas. With so much in between, it was a feather-like touch. But that made it even more enticing.

"The easy route begins here." He traced his finger in a horizontal motion to the other thigh and moved once again toward her center, then back across and down the other leg. "And that leaves only six turns to get to the center and then six back out again."

She couldn't speak. She wasn't following the route at all. All she could think about was the rising heat in her core and the pulsing need for him at this moment. She leaned in and ran her hands along his bare arms. She moved the paper to the side table and scooted into his lap, her legs wrapped around him. She took his face in her hands and, with eyes wide open, kissed him with all the passion she held inside. Before she knew what she was doing, she moved into his lap to satiate the pulsing between her legs.

He growled against her mouth, and returned her kisses with an exciting combination of assertiveness and softness. "Sarah... I...What do..."

She moved against him more and felt his hardness. "Please," she said. "I can't stand it anymore. I want all of you."

He stood with her wrapped around him, still kissing her and one arm supporting her weight as he quickly strode back into the house and toward her bedroom. Her mouth never left his. She wanted to absorb all his energy, his total being, to be one with him in both a physical and psychic way.

As he lowered her to the bed, he fingered open her robe and laid it to each side, exposing the small camisole and shorts she wore beneath it. He stripped off his own t-shirt and ran his fingers along all the edges of the two pieces she wore. He gently raised her toward him to remove the robe. She marveled again at his muscled chest and stomach.

She hadn't seen his chest in months. It seemed like years ago that they had played in the mud while planting the crops. His hands moved up her legs and he gently separated them. His lips followed up one leg and down the other, making her want him even more. "Please," she said again. She wanted him on top of her, to the side of her, all around her, inside her.

He straddled her and as his lips moved gently from one eye to the other, down to the tip of her nose and across to each cheek. His hands stroked her hair, swept gently across her shoulders, ending with his fingertips tracking down her arms. Then his lips followed all those places he'd touched. Finally, he recaptured her mouth. As their tongues tangled she arched toward him and moved against him in a frenzy

When his hands moved beneath her camisole and cupped a breast in one hand, her eyes flew open in surprise. He recaptured her mouth again and she was lost in him. Their bodies moving as one, she felt his full weight and the brush of the soft jersey pajama bottoms against her stomach. That softness contrasted with the naked, muscled arms looming above her. She couldn't help but follow every contour with her fingers.

His fingers worked to the side of her shorts and he ran them along the leg cuffs skimming her most private area. He grasped the top of the shorts to work them off her.

"Are you sure, Sarah?" he asked, his breathing ragged. "You need to be sure. You need to want this as much as I do, no regrets."

She wasn't sure. All she knew was that she needed him with every fiber of her being. She stroked her hands along his side, reached for him and brought his full weight on top of her, kissing him hard.

"Sarah?" he asked again.

"I don't know!" she cried out. "I want you so much. I've never felt like this." She moved against him and he backed off, holding himself above her.

"I can satisfy your need without making love to you, Sarah." She shivered in the loss of his weight and warmth. "If you aren't sure, I can stop now and help this need go away. I don't want you to regret this moment because we aren't married yet."

Her mind was a swirl of emotion. She wanted him. She needed him. She loved him. They were going to be married anyway in six short weeks. And she knew now, in the most painful way possible, that life could change—be ended—in an instant. She no longer wanted to be the twenty-eight year old virgin, too scared of these emotions that threatened to encompass her. She wanted all the beauty and pleasure life had to offer. Including Tom.

"Yes!" she said. "I want this." To prove it she quickly removed her camisole and shorts. "Hurry, I'm cold."

He laughed as he shucked his pajama bottoms. "I love you, Sarah. I love you."

With each move they made she became more sure and more in love as they synched with each other. When they finally joined it was overwhelming and wonderful and scary and amazing and loving all at the same time. She gave up on trying to capture the memory, as all she could do was feel and react and finally…shatter into a million stars.

SHE WASN'T sure how long they stayed in each other's arms, before hearing voices in the living room.

"No!" Connor said. "Don't bother them."

"But I need to see if Daddy is in there," Grady whined. "I want breakfast."

"He's in there," Connor said.

"How do you know?"

"I just do. Come on, I'll fix some toast."

"But I want pancakes. We get pancakes on Saturday."

Big sigh. "Toast first, then when Daddy wakes up we'll get pancakes."

Then quiet.

Tom pulled her close. Brushed her lips, then each eye and her forehead. "Welcome to parenthood." He smiled and then kissed her again. This time more deeply. "I'll jump in the shower and then get breakfast started. You take your time."

He rolled off the bed, and for the first time she saw him completely naked and her eyes grew wide. He smiled, leaned over and kissed her again. "I'm thinking I better move my things in here from now on." Then he turned, donned his pajama bottoms and quietly walked out the door.

Dear Lord, what had she done? She searched her heart for guilt or regret, but didn't find any. Nothing they did last night felt wrong. In fact it all felt very right and long overdue. She stretched languorously, basking in the sleep-filled peace instilled by pure satisfaction.

By the time Sarah got out of bed, showered, and dressed the boys had been fed, the dishes cleaned, and they were already outside with Tom helping set up the maze for Halloween.

She stood on the porch debating whether to join them or let them have their bonding time with Tom. He was such a good man. Somehow, in the intervening eight years, he had become the man she knew was buried deep inside when she first fell in love with him.

And this morning...she was unable to stop smiling. Did she want Tom in her bed every night now? Yes...and no. It was all so new—scary and amazing at the same time. She was afraid she might not get out of bed for the entire six weeks before the wedding. She laughed at herself. Did all women feel this way the first time they made love? That feeling that it was hard to tell where one body started and the other ended. That feeling that went beyond the physical sensations and called to the spiritual love in their souls to be forever bonded. When he had left the bed, she felt as if a part of her was missing. She wanted to follow him to the shower and start all over again.

Of course, when they were married they would share the same bed every night. But that would be different. Wouldn't it? She couldn't imagine feeling this way every time. It would be exhausting!

She shook her head then made a decision. As much as she loved what happened last night, she would ask Tom to wait until their honeymoon. There was so much to explore about this passion they held for each other. She wanted to do that when they had uninterrupted time together. Not worry about the boys walking in. No second thoughts about luxuriating in the carnal side of their love. No need to get out of bed at any particular time.

She forced herself to stop reliving those moments in her head. She'd have to be careful when she was around her Sweetwater Canyon friends. Especially Rachel. If Rachel found out she'd be grilling Sarah for every last detail. And that was something she didn't want. She wanted to hold these moments to herself. This first time would always be a special secret between her and Tom to hold in their hearts.

Just then her cell phone rang. She saw Rachel's name displayed on the phone. She looked up to the sky. "Really? You're going to test me on this right now?"

She took a deep breath and swiped the answer button. "Hi, Rache. What's up?"

"Did you forget we're all going shopping for your wedding dress today?"

"Oh, no! I did!" With everything that happened this morning, she wasn't completely sure of the day or time.

"Not having second thoughts are you?"

"No! Definitely not," Sarah answered quickly. "What time is it?"

"Eleven-thirty. You said you'd call by ten to let us know when to pick you up. Everything okay?"

"Just got busy around the farm." She blushed. Thank goodness they weren't doing face time on this. "Come on over. I'm dressed and everything."

"You're dressed?" Rachel asked. "Why wouldn't you be dressed at eleven-thirty in the morning? You're always an early riser."

Rachel was silent for a moment, and then Sarah heard laughter bubbling and getting louder and louder.

"I can't friggin' believe it!" Rachel said. "You finally did it, didn't you? You just got out of bed after making love all night, didn't you? Was it amazing? How many times? Was he careful with you? Of course he was. Tom is a great man and he would never hurt you. Are you too tired to go out? If so, you can tell me. I'll explain to everyone why we have to wait for tomorrow. That would give you time to go back to bed for a nooner. Oh my god, they are all going to be thrilled!

"If you could just see me now. I'm dancing in the yard of the B&B. I'm so happy for you. Finally! Wow! I can't wait to tell Michele and Theresa. Not sure if I should tell Kat. Wait, of course, Kat should be told. She's like a sister to us.

"I can't believe it. Saint Sarah finally got laid!"

Sarah could barely speak. She was mortified that Rachel had guessed, even though the exact details were different. And she definitely didn't want anyone to know—especially not Kat. Kat wasn't even eighteen yet.

"It's not...how you said," she finally got out before Rachel could embellish her fantasy even more. "We did not make love all night. I don't have the energy for that."

"But you had more energy then you thought, right? The time or length doesn't matter as long as it was good." She laughed. "It *was* good, right?"

The guilt Sarah hadn't felt before was now raising its ugly head. What kind of example was she setting? Especially for Kat. Sarah had hoped that waiting, even when she really loved Tom, was a way to help Kat understand that she could wait in the future too, and that sex shouldn't be forced.

Sarah had endured Rachel's teasing for years as she held on so voraciously to her values about no sex before marriage. And now she was an example of failure instead of strength.

She was just like everyone else.

"Sarah?" Rachel's voice sounded concerned. "I'm sorry. I shouldn't tease. You know me. I can be wretched some times. It's just that I never understood the whole virgin thing. You know me, before Noel I was testing out every guy I fancied and even some I didn't."

Sarah shook her head in defeat. "I know. I never meant to act like I was a saint," she finally said. "I admit it. Yes, Tom and I made love...

but not all night. I couldn't wait even five more weeks. That's how weak I am."

"Oh cack!" Rachel said. "Now I've gone and tainted it for you."

"No. You're fine. It's me. I'm just mad at me for not waiting. "

"Listen, Sarah. I'm sorry. I shouldn't have pushed. You are *not* a sinner. You did what anyone in love does. You just held out a lot longer than most people."

"I was so self-righteous about it though, wasn't I?" Sarah asked.

"You had your reasons," Rachel said. "Do you know that Noel is the only guy who ever refused me? And believe me I was offering within a week of us meeting. Offering again and again, but he turned me down. Even though he loved me, he wanted to make sure it was more than lust, more than me needing comfort or self-assurance. That's true love. That's the kind of love that makes for forever and makes it special when it finally happens. Don't let my ramblings make something ugly out of something beautiful between you and Tom. It was beautiful, wasn't it?"

"Yes…but…"

"No buts," Rachel pronounced. "Now, I'm going to get Michele and Theresa and pick you up so we can at least find a wedding dress before the next time you want to jump the bones of your man."

"Rache, please don't tell…"

"No worries. This is just between you and me. Our secret. I promise. I'm just so happy for you, Sarah. After all you've been through you deserve this. Really, you deserve a good man like Tom. Don't go feeling bad about this. I'm sure God is happy for you too."

Sarah wasn't so sure God understood. There was a good reason for rules, for faithfulness. She had been sure God understood before talking to Rachel, but now she wondered if it had been wishful thinking.

"We'll be there in fifteen."

Sarah hung up the phone and wrapped her arms around herself. She'd been feeling so good this morning—so guilt free and happy. And now…well it definitely shined a bright light of reality on her decision. She and Tom would not make love again until they were married and he definitely was *not* going to be moving into the bedroom until after the honeymoon.

∼

"ARE you sure you want something this simple?" Kat asked. "When I get married, I want to be Belle from Beauty and the Beast, like a princess. This is pretty but more like hippie-dippy farm girl gets married in a shack."

Sarah laughed. "I am a farm girl. Not sure about the hippie part. And we are getting married on the front porch of our home. It's not quite a shack, but it's no castle either."

She'd never been a dress-up kind of girl. She'd grown up on the farm where she and Tom were living. Even when she played with the band, her dress-up outfit was dark jeans and a white, collared shirt with a dark blue or black vest. She did have four or five vests to change up the colors. A couple of them even had subtle small flower prints.

Sarah fingered the soft cotton of the floor-length gown. She loved the v-neck in the front that was not too low but also not overly modest. And the shirring of the top added definition to her small breasts and tapered to define her waist. The small amount of lace that bordered the neckline and the cap sleeves was enough to make it feel special—more than a dress one would wear to a garden party or to church.

The ease of the flare of the skirt from the waist to the floor was just enough to show her figure but not body hugging. She turned and held up a mirror so she could see the back of the dress at full length. The vee repeated in the back, edged with tulle and lace, exposing just enough skin to be interesting but not flaunting her sexuality. She could already imagine the heat of Tom's hand touching a small part of her bare skin and reminding her of what they'd shared.

She closed her eyes a moment and took a breath, not wanting to get lost again in those feelings with her best friends watching her every move.

"Let me fix this," Kat said. Sarah felt her fiddling with the bow on the back of the dress. "This is a lot of material and it has to be done just right."

Sarah held the hand mirror at an angle to watch as Kat pulled the wide satin ribbon a little tighter around the waist before expertly tying the bow so that the two tails hung flat and the bow was perfectly horizontal. Then she worked her fingers under each pouf to make it stand on its own without wrinkles.

"It's perfect," Sarah said. "Thank goodness you will be in the bedroom to help me dress."

The shop owner stepped up to the group and examined the fit. "Good," she muttered as she checked the way the top lay against her body. Then she bent to the hem. "Put on the shoes you are going to wear."

Sarah slipped into a basic white, one-inch pump.

"Do a little twirl," the owner said. Sarah complied. "Good. Can you walk in it without tripping?"

Sarah walked to the front door and back. It didn't hamper her stride at all and she didn't feel it brushing the floor.

"Perfect for a garden wedding," the woman pronounced. "You have the perfect body and height for this dress. I've never had a bride who needed no alterations. This is a good sign for this union."

Sarah smiled. Everything was good today.

Kat grabbed a short veil off the rack near the mirrors and draped it over Sarah's head. "How about this? It adds more sparkle."

Sarah looked in the mirror. Too much sparkle. It had little rhinestones all over the tulle. She carefully removed it and handed it back. "Just not me, Kat."

"Right. I forgot. Hippie dippy farm girl." Next Kat reached for a more understated floral head wreath adorned with silk roses in a dusty antique blush. It also contained dried, ivory star flowers and faux Queen Anne's lace. She secured it to the top of Sarah's head with hairpins. "This is more the boho look you seem to like."

Sarah looked in the mirror "It's pretty and definitely more my style. But with my short hair I think it kind of takes over. If my hair were still long, it would be perfect."

"I know just the thing," Rachel said and she almost skipped toward the front of the store. She returned with a delicate, double-rowed headband with small faux white pearls interspersed with a dark mahogany stone. The pearls and stones were not prolific, covering the whole headband. Rather they were distinctive with good spacing between them.

Rachel carefully worked the headband onto Sarah's scalp. "What do you think?"

Sarah turned again to the mirror. Her eyes misted. "It's ...perfect." It was just the right statement for her pixie hair and it was simple enough to go with the cotton and lace gown and still be special.

"Wow!" Kat said. "You're right. It's perfect for Sarah."

"With the autumn flowers from your garden as part of the bouquet everything will be beautiful," Michele said. "Tom will be flabbergasted. He won't be able to say his vows because he'll be looking at you the whole time."

"Theresa?" Sarah asked, turning to her standing slightly outside of the circle of friends.

Theresa held up her finger and nodded. Sarah could see a tear slip down her face.

"I know you're not my daughter," Theresa said. "But I feel like you are. Everything you've been through...I'm just so happy for you."

All three women gathered around and hugged her at once.

"Let's move up the wedding and get Sarah married today." Kat said. "I don't think I can wait five more weeks to see her walk down the aisle."

"You don't know the half of it," Rachel said.

Sarah sent her a warning look.

"I mean...when Noel and I got married all I could think about was how quickly he could get me out of my gown. It's good this one is simple. Tom won't have to think too hard."

They all laughed.

"That's all you think about," Michele said. "Sex and more sex."

"And your point is?" Rachel asked, a roguish grin on her face. "Obviously, you and David rarely give it a break. With two kids already, and the pounding I hear in the next room, I'd say a day rarely passes without sex."

Michele made a fist and playfully punched Rachel's upper arm. "You know that's not true. David hasn't been here in the past week."

"He hasn't?" Rachel asked. "Then it's all phone sex I'm hearing?"

"Now, now," Theresa intervened. "Let's not embarrass Sarah with all this talk of sex."

"It's okay," Sarah said. For once she actually understood why Rachel loved sex so much. "I've missed you and your teasing. You've all been so careful around me since I got out of the hospital three months ago."

"Well," Theresa shifted her weight from one foot to the other. "I guess you're good then." She moved behind Sarah and pulled the bow open. "Let's get you out of this and get this packaged, paid for, and put in a garment bag so we can finish our shopping."

"You are going to be the most beautiful bride on your special day," Kat said. "Michele is right. Tom won't be able to speak." I hope one day I find someone as wonderful as him.

"You will, honey. You will," Theresa promised. "Just don't be in a rush. Let's at least get you off to college." Theresa gave Sarah a push toward the dressing room. "Go on and get changed. Rachel, you help her." She looked at her watch. "I rescheduled the caterer for the tasting from the original one-thirty time to two-thirty and we can't be late."

"Oooo. Food!" Kat said. "How could I have forgotten about that? And we never got lunch."

Sarah walked slowly toward the dressing room. Everything was so wonderful right now. Her best friends were laughing and teasing again. She'd found the perfect wedding dress. For a moment she considered retying the bow, calling Tom, and running over to the church to meet him.

No more planning. No more waiting.

She sighed and stepped back into the dressing room. Five more weeks wasn't so bad. Compared to eight years, it was nothing.

CHAPTER 6

"$\mathcal{D}$id you have fun?" Tom asked when the four of them sat down for dinner together.

"Can I see your wedding gown?" Connor asked. "I know Daddy can't see it, but I can, right? I bet you are beautiful. Is it fancy?"

"Me too, me too!" Grady yelled. "I wanna see it too."

"It's a surprise for everybody," Sarah said.

"But Miss Rachel, and Miss Kat, and Miss Theresa saw it right?" Connor countered.

"Yes, they helped me pick it out."

"Then it's not a surprise to everybody." He emphasized the last word with sarcasm.

Sarah laughed. "You're right. It's just a surprise to the boys."

"Is that right, Daddy?" Grady asked. "Why do boys have to wait? That's not fair."

Tom put his arm across Grady's shoulder. "That's just the tradition for probably a hundred years. The girl picks it out and doesn't show it to any boys until the wedding day. I don't know why, it's just the way it is."

"Geez. That's not fair," Grady said.

"When you get married, maybe you can change the rules. That is if you can get the girl to agree." Tom pointed at the peas still on Grady's plate. "Don't forget to finish these or you'll never be strong enough to get married."

"Really? Peas make you strong? I thought it was only spinach."

"All vegetables make you strong," Connor said with confidence. "That's what Dad...I mean..." He looked up at Tom.

"Yes," Tom said. "I remember your dad used to say that all the time. And he knew what he was talking about. He was one of the best farmers in all of Broken Bow. I feel fortunate to have known him. He taught me a lot too."

Connor tried to smile, though his lip trembled. "I'm sorry. I got confused."

"Don't be sorry, Connor," Tom said softly. "Lots of kids have two dads. You can love both of us at the same time. Just because he's not with us anymore, doesn't mean you don't love him. I don't ever want you to forget what a wonderful man and father he was."

Sarah reached across to touch Tom's hand. It was times like these she had little doubt that the four of them as a family was definitely in God's plan. Tom was so good with the boys. There would be a lot of ups and downs, but together they would make this work.

Tom took her hand fully in his and squeezed. She couldn't stop looking at him.

"Uh-oh," Grady said. "They are doing that staring thing where they look like their going to kiss."

"Kiss. Kiss. Kiss." Connor started the chant and Grady joined in. "Kiss. Kiss. Kiss."

Sarah and Tom stood and leaned across the table for a quick, chaste kiss.

"Yay!" Both boys exclaimed.

"See," Grady said. "They still love each other. I told you!"

"Who wants dessert?" Sarah asked as she picked up the dinner dishes. "We have vanilla ice cream and, while I was out shopping for my dress, I picked up some chocolate fudge syrup to put on top of it."

"And bananas too?" Connor asked, eyes wide."

"Yes, and bananas too."

"Sundaes!" Both boys jumped up, and quickly helped to clear the table. They practically ran with the dishes into the kitchen.

"Slow down," Tom cautioned. "We don't want to have to buy new dishes."

A chime bonged three times and then repeated. Sarah looked around the room.

"That's your phone," Tom said.

"Oh, right." She pulled it from her pants pocked and looked at the number, but didn't recognize it. It looked like an Oklahoma City area code. Who would call from Oklahoma City? "Probably someone trying to sell something," she said aloud.

"Then don't answer it" Tom said. "If it's important they'll call you back."

Too late, she'd already automatically swiped it to answer. "Hello."

"Is this Sarah?"

"Yes. And you are?" Sarah asked.

"You don't know me, but I'm a friend of Amanda."

"Amanda Davidson?" Sarah said loud enough for Tom to hear.

Tom stepped to her side, a stack of plates in his hands and raised an eyebrow in question.

"Yes. Please don't hang up," the woman's voice quickly inserted.

"She can't call you directly from prison...because of what she did to you...but she asked me to call you. She wants to apologize for everything she's done. Will you accept the call?"

Sarah froze. She couldn't speak.

"Hang up." Tom grabbed for her phone but she held it tight to her chest. "Hang. Up!"

"I can't," Sarah said, her voice shaking as she put the phone back to her ear.

"Please accept," the woman said. "It's just an apology."

"Ye-eh-es," She choked out in response. Sarah had been praying for an opportunity like this—an opportunity for the boys to maintain a loving relationship with their mother, even if Amanda was going to be in prison the rest of her life.

Tom shook his head violently from side to side. "Sarah, what are you doing?"

Sarah covered the phone with a hand and whispered,"I have to do this. I have everything I've ever wanted. And she has *nothing* now. I think…I've made mistakes in my past, yet God has forgiven me. I need to give Amanda at least one chance to do the right thing. A chance at redemption." She pushed Tom toward the kitchen. "Go. Go do sundaes with the boys."

Tom hesitated.

"Tom?" Amanda's voice oozed over the phone.

"No. This is Sarah. How are you doing, Amanda?"

Tom stomped toward the kitchen.

"Is Tom there?"

"He can't talk right now," Sarah said. "The woman said you wanted to talk to me. Something about an apology?"

"Oh. I…"

After a long pause, Sarah asked, "Are you doing better now? Are you getting help?"

Another long pause left Sarah wondering if Amanda would choose not to talk to her at all.

"I…I'm…sorry for what I did," Amanda said, her voice hesitant. "I don't know what happened. I must have gone crazy with grief over Henry's death. It seems that ever since he died, I wasn't myself."

"He didn't just die, Amanda. You killed him," Sarah said, and waited for Amanda's acknowledgement. When she didn't hear one, she continued. "I want to help you. I want to help you have a loving relationship with Connor and Grady. But I can't do that if you don't take responsibility for killing their father."

"Right. Of course, you're right. I uh…it's hard to imagine why I did that. I just kin of lost it. I definitely want Connor and Grady to know I love them."

"I'm so glad to hear that!" Sarah was now sure it was the right thing to take this call. "They are so confused…and hurt around everything that has happened. Knowing you didn't abandon them on purpose is the first step toward rebuilding a relationship with them."

"Um…yeah…I guess I did kill Henry. I mean I didn't plan on it. Actually, I don't remember it. Not really. But the proof is pretty hard to deny. That's why I'm in here, right? Well, that and how awful I treated you. I'm sorry about that too."

"Are you truly sorry, Amanda? I'm not sure you completely understand how everything you did affects your children.

Silence.

Sarah didn't say anything either. She knew Amanda needed time think about what happened before she could take responsibility. Sarah could be patient. Maybe it would take more than one phone call to work this out.

"Um…" Amanda's voice came back on the line. "I'm pretty sure that the whole thing with Henry was the beginning of my…uh… psychotic breakdown. I mean I know I kidnapped you and stuff, but… whatever happened at the cabin, that wasn't the real me. You understand that, right? That wasn't me. I was, like, a different person. Like satan walked into me and did all those things."

"I've been praying for your healing," Sarah said quietly. She wasn't hearing what she'd hoped. She knew Amanda brought up satan as a way to excuse her actions. That wasn't the way it worked.

Sarah had practiced this conversation in her mind for the past three months. Amanda would apologize and tell her she'd changed her ways and was getting help with her obsession with Tom. Sarah would say she forgave her and they would set up a series of calls to help her keep in touch with the boys. And then Sarah could put this bad piece of her life behind her. Together, she and Tom would raise the boys and still provide them some quality time with their mother. Sarah didn't ever want to worry again about Amanda taking over their lives.

Tom had said when bad things happen you have to give meaning to them and move on. Maybe the meaning of this was for Amanda to reconnect with her children—to be a part of their healing too. Then Sarah could believe everything she went through had been worth it.

"Thank you, Sarah." Amanda finally broke the silence. "I'm sure your prayers are helping." Sarah could hear Amanda drumming her fingers on a desk or a wall. "Um…when will Tom be back? I need to ask him something. Something you wouldn't know about. It's about Connor and Grady."

"They are doing fine," Sarah said. "Considering all that happened."

"Do they know…I'm in prison?"

"Connor does," she answered honestly. "He saw you kill Henry. He will never get that image out of his mind. The only way he could feel safe is to know you wouldn't come after him and Grady too."

"I would never do that," Amanda's voice actually sounded like she might be crying. "I would never hurt my babies."

Sarah was starting to question her plan to help Amanda build any kind of relationship with her children. She seemed oblivious to her behavior with all the other men in town and leaving the boys for months on end with only Henry to care for them.

"What about Grady?" Amanda asked. "Does he know?"

"No, we haven't told him. He's too young to understand. We've just said that you are gone for a long time and that is why we are caring for them."

"We?"

"Tom and I. Tom has guardianship as Henry set up in his will. When we get married, we will adopt them."

"What!" Amanda's voice shrilled. Sarah held the phone away from her ear. "No! No, you are *not* allowed to be a mother to my children!"

"Mommy?"

She hadn't notice Grady step into the room.

Grady hurried to Sarah's side and reached for the phone. "Is that my Mommy on the phone? I wanna talk to her."

"I'm here, Grady!" Amanda screamed through the phone. "Mommy loves you! Not Sarah. Sarah doesn't love you! She's hiding you from me. Only Mr. Tom loves you."

Sarah switched off the phone in horror and put it in her pocket.

"Mommy?" Grady tried to get the phone out of Sarah's pocket, but Sarah placed her hand over it.

Sarah bent over, gently putting her hands on Grady's shoulders. "She can't talk to you right now, sweetie."

"Call her back. She's scared. She wanted to talk to me. You hung up. I *need* to talk to her."

"I'm sorry, honey, you can't. Your mommy is very sick, and she doesn't always know what she's saying. She is not allowed to talk to you."

Grady's lower lip jutted out and his breaths came in short spurts as he pushed air through his nose. "Where is she?" His breathing caught and started again. "Is she in the hospital like you? If she's sick I have to go to see her." Tears choked his words. "I have to help make her better."

"She's…um…in a place kind of like a hospital—a place where you can't visit until your older."

"No!" He shouted. "I don't believe you. You call her back. Now! Call her back!" With tears streaming down his face, he flailed clenched fists at Sarah's thigh. "She needs my help. Where is she? I don't want her to die too. I don't want anyone else to die. I need to tell her I love her. Please call her back. Pleeeeaaaaase." He begged.

Tom and Connor appeared in the doorway.

"What's wrong?" Tom asked.

"Miss Sarah won't call Mommy back," Grady still couldn't catch his breath as he spoke. "She wants to come home. She misses me. Call her back. Call her back. Daddy, make Miss Sarah call her back."

Grady slumped onto the floor and Tom picked him up and rocked him.

"See what you've done?" Tom whispered.

Sarah's own tears could no longer be held in. How could she have misinterpreted Amanda's call as God's answer to her prayers? All the work she'd done to make this a whole family was now undone by her one selfish act of trying to put the past behind her at any cost.

"Daddy, call her back," Grady said between tears, his whole body shaking as he spoke. "Miss Sarah hates Mommy. She won't call her back."

"Grady, I don't hate your mother. I told you that she needs help. The doctors are trying to help her get better."

Sarah noticed Connor standing straight as a board against the opposite wall and swallowing repeatedly. She was sure this was bothering him as much as Grady, but she could only deal with one child at a time.

"I thought you loved us," Grady said.

"I do!" she said fiercely.

"Then you need to help Mommy come home."

"Stop it!" Connor yelled. "She can't come home because she's in prison. She killed Daddy!"

Sarah froze. It was as if time stood still and all her worse fears about her ability to help raise these children came true at once.

Grady twisted in Tom's lap, half standing as he yelled to Connor. "You're lying. Take it back. Take it back!"

"No I'm not! I saw her do it! Mommy is very bad. You can never see her. You can never trust her."

"No! She said she loves me. I want to see her! I want to see her now!" Grady managed to escape from Tom's grasp and ran out of the room.

"With one phone call, you've ruined three months of work." Tom spat out the words. He turned and rushed toward the boys' bedroom.

Sarah looked at Connor, now slumped in the corner almost curled into a fetal ball.

"I'm so sorry, Connor. I'm so sorry. I didn't know. I thought she'd already had time to get help, to get better."

"It's all right Miss Sarah," Connor whispered. "It's not your fault."

"Yes, it is. I should have listened to Tom. I should have…"

Connor scooted toward her and wrapped his small arms around her waist. "My counselor said Mommy will never stop being bad because she's sick. She has absession. Do you know what that is?"

"Yes. You mean obsession."

"That's right. I remember now. Her obsession makes it so she can't see anything except the one thing she wants. And that means you can never trust her and she will never be able to be the mommy I want."

"Your counselor is very smart," Sarah said, amazed at how far Connor had come from the constantly scared little boy who had clung to Tom like a two-year-old.

"It makes me sad," Connor sad. "But it makes me safe too. If I don't talk to her I won't be confused. That's why you can't talk to her either. 'Cause she knows how to lie to make people confused."

Sarah nodded her head. Maybe she should find a counselor too. How could she be the parent these boys needed when Connor had more sense than she did?

"Thank you, Connor. You are very wise for being only seven years old." She hugged him back.

"Sarah! Connor!" Tom ran from outside back into the living room. He was breathing hard as if he'd been running for a long time. "Did Grady come through here?"

Sarah stood quickly. "No. I thought he went to his room. I thought you've been talking to him all this time."

"He wasn't in his room," Tom said between labored breaths. "I assumed he ran outside to work off his tantrum. But I've called and he doesn't answer. I checked the barn. That's where he usually goes and talks to Kip or the horses. But he's not there, and neither is Kip."

Sarah gasped. If the border collie was gone, it meant Grady had run away. He'd never done that before. But Sarah understood the urge. That's what she did as a child whenever she got really mad at her father.

Sarah looked at Connor. "Where would he go?"

"I don't know," Connor said, his voice tired. "You've already checked the barn. Don't worry. He'll come back. He always does. He used to do this all the time whenever Mom lied to us. He hates lies."

"Please think, Connor," Sarah said. "I know you've had a rough day, thanks to me. But it's dark outside. Grady could fall and get hurt. He could be bleeding or wander on the road and get hit by a car. Or—"

Tom grasped her shoulders and shook her lightly. "Stop."

Sarah nodded and drew in a big breath.

Tom knelt in front of Connor. "You're probably right that he will come back on his own, but we still need to look for him."

"I'll show you all his hiding places," Connor said.

"Good. Put your boots on, we may be tramping through a lot of bushes and dirt."

While Connor ran to his bedroom, Sarah stepped on the porch and fetched her own boots.

Tom stayed her hand. "Sarah, you stay here in case he comes back to the house. I don't want him leaving again to find us."

"I'm not sure he'll come back with me here," she said miserably. "Amanda will never stop harassing you or the boys until I leave."

He grabbed her shoulders and held her still. His jaw and lips were like stone, unmoving. His eyes widened but his brows drew together. She wasn't sure if he was angry or scared. "Don't go there," he said through locked teeth. "We need you. We need you right here, right now, with us. If Grady comes back, he will be tired and all run out. You will know what to do. You always do."

"Evidently, not always." She hung her head. "I was so sure of myself."

Connor ran back to the porch with his boots on.

"We can't discuss this right now," Tom said. "You can do this. Just stay here and be ready."

She nodded as Tom and Connor bounded down the stairs and disappeared into the dark night. She followed the light of their bouncing flashlights as they jogged across the field, calling Grady's name.

When she could no longer hear them or see their light, she looked up to the starry sky and prayed.

Please, Father. Please keep Grady safe. Once again, I didn't listen to others. Tom told me to hang up. Yet I refused. Once again, I let my belief in what's right – I let my pride dictate the plan. Please don't punish Grady for my mistakes. Please bring him back to us unharmed.

AFTER NEARLY TWO hours of searching the property, Tom and Connor returned.

"I don't know where he is," Tom said. "I think it's time we called the police. I don't know if he's hiding from us and safe, or if he's hurt lying in a ditch somewhere."

Tom pulled out his cell phone and it rang.

"It's the Rogers," he said to Sarah and Connor. "Hello?" He listened a moment. "Thank God!" He sank next to Sarah on the sofa and pulled Connor to him. "Yes. Yes, I understand. I'll come then. Thank you. Thank you for taking care of him."

"They have him?" Sarah asked, praying at the same time it wasn't an illusion.

"Yes, he walked all the way there—three miles—and knocked on the door. He asked if he could live with them again because he didn't want to live here anymore."

"Let's go get him then," Sarah said. "I'll get some blankets and a pillow."

Tom stopped her from moving off the sofa. "Not tonight. The Rogers have already put him to bed. They suggested I come first thing in the morning and have breakfast with them."

"That's a good idea. Let him sleep off his anger."

"That's not all," Tom said. He placed a hand softly on her arm. "Grady said...He told the Rogers...he wouldn't come home if you were here." He turned toward her. "Remember, this is a scared, confused child.

"What. Did, He. Say?" Sarah asked, her voice shaking.

"He said that you were a liar. That you didn't really love him."

Her heart seemed to stop in her chest. In the silence, she felt her lungs straining to take the next breath. She wasn't sure that next beat would come and release her from the consequences of her mistake.

"I...I see." She said the words on an inhale that forced her heart to beat out the agony of what was to come.

Tom took her in his full embrace and rocked her. "No, you don't see. This is a four-year-old who is confused and angry. He has to blame someone and right now that's you. By the end of tomorrow it may be me."

"Of course," she said, her brain shutting down emotion before it engulfed her. "You're right. I'll…I'll call Michele…or Theresa…or…" She wiped at her face as tears formed unbidden. "They'll take me to the hotel. You can talk to Grady and then let me know when it's safe to come home."

Connor crawled onto the sofa on Sarah's other side, adding his hug to Tom's. "Miss Sarah. I mean…Mommy," he said. "It will work out. You'll see. We can still be a family. You saved us. You and Mr. Tom. I mean Daddy. Don't worry, Grady will understand. Then you can save us again."

Sarah nodded, unable to speak. She softly pushed out of their embrace and stood. She balanced her hand on the back of the sofa, afraid if she moved too quickly she might fall over and never get up again.

"You don't have to go tonight, Sarah. You can get a good night's sleep and go in the morning."

"No," she said, as she turned toward her bedroom. "I'll go tonight. I don't want anything else to go wrong."

"Sarah." Tom grabbed her arm to stop her.

She looked down at his hand. "I need some time. Alone." He didn't let go. She couldn't fight now. She could barely stand. "Please."

Tom swallowed hard and released her.

"I'll put Connor to bed and then I'll come help you pack."

"I'll be fine." She bent toward Connor. "Connor, no matter what happens I want you to know that I love you and Grady forever. Do you understand that?"

Connor's eyes widened.

"I will make sure you are all safe, and strong, and happy. I promise."

Then she gave him a kiss on his cheek and moved slowly down the hallway to her bedroom. It took every bit of willpower to not look back.

As she closed the door she heard Connor ask, "Is she going to be okay, Daddy? She seemed very sad."

"Yes," Tom said. "Don't worry about Miss Sarah. She has a faith stronger than ten men combined."

"Are you still getting married?"

"Of course we are. We love each other very much, and we both love you and Grady. We will all figure this out together and, when Miss Sarah comes back, we will be a real family. That's what families do. They figure things out together."

She closed the door, not able to listen anymore. What did she know about family? Her mother died when she was eight. Her father was an alcoholic. Though he loved her, he was not an example of what she imagined was a real family.

She dialed Theresa's number. She figured she'd start there. She had no doubt they'd come—probably all of them. The Sweetwater Canyon band was the closest thing to a family she'd ever known. She'd be safe with them.

CHAPTER 7

*S*arah stretched carefully in the bed, slowly unwinding her body from a small corner of the bed near the wall. How she ended up in a small ball when she had the entire queen bed to herself was a mystery. She rolled to face away from the wall and peered beneath her lashes to see if anyone else in the room was still sleeping. Hearing no one breathing, she reached toward the bed stand clock.

Nine-thirty! She sat up instantly. Why did they let her sleep so late?

Last night's move to the extended stay hotel had been smooth but exhausting. She'd been so emotional about everything she could barely string two coherent sentences together. In the end her brain simply stopped taking in any information. So she went straight to bed around ten-thirty last night.

The two-bedroom suite had two bedrooms separated by a shared living room. Each bedroom held two queen beds. She'd been given the second bed in the suite with Theresa, and Kat ended up with the sleeper sofa in the living room. Michele and Rachel shared the other bedroom. Though Kat was gracious about the whole thing, Sarah felt it wasn't fair to put Kat out of her bed. But Theresa wouldn't hear of Sarah using the sleeper sofa.

Sarah popped into the bathroom for a shower and found a sticky note tacked to the mirror.

Hope you slept well. We are across the street at the Cowbell Café having a late breakfast. Come join us when you wake up. We promise not to ask questions this time.

Someone had added the time as 10 a.m. in different colored ink. If she hurried in the shower, she wouldn't be too late.

~

SARAH TOOK a deep breath as she opened the door to the Cowbell Café. She'd been coming here for breakfast since she was a small child. Once a month her mom and dad would make a family brunch day after church on Sunday morning. They always ordered the home-made pancakes. Dad ordered the tall stack, plain with maple syrup. Mom ordered a single pancake with whipped cream and raspberries or blueberries, and Sarah got the short stack—two pancakes with Mrs. Carter's special touch.

The owner would make sure to draw a cow face in powdered sugar on top of Sarah's stack. She would depict the dark eyes with two blackberries, and the ear tag was always a small square of dark choco-late. She could still remember the heavenly taste of syrup over the pancakes as it combined with the powdered sugar and chocolate.

In fact, her last happy memory of her mother was here at the café. Sarah knew about ear tags for cattle, but her child logic saw them more as decoration than a way to differentiate cows from neighboring farms. She thought of the tabs as cow earrings, and complained that it looked unbalanced to have only one. The last few months of her mother's life, she had taken to sneaking an extra piece of chocolate on to the other ear. Mrs. Carter never delivered the pancakes with two chocolates, only one.

After they thanked God for the meal, Sarah would open her eyes and see the other cow ear adorned. She knew it was her mother doing this but she could never catch her at it. Even if she opened her eyes during the prayer, she never saw her mother place it on the pancake.

Those kind of small gestures of love helped build Sarah's confidence. It set a foundation for her expectations of family. That was a long time ago. After her mother's death, she soon learned what an anomaly that type of unconditional love had been.

"Sarah, back here." She heard Kat's voice above the low din of the air conditioner. Kat waved from the back of the restaurant and pointed at an empty chair at their table.

Sarah slowly wound her way past tables filled with couples and families. It seemed the café still packed in both locals and visitors on the weekends. Not much had changed.

The décor was still kitschy with the dairy farm mural wallpaper on one side of the restaurant. A plethora of small wooden shelves dotted the opposite wall. Each shelf just large enough to hold a single cowbell, each one different—some antiques, some with advertising, some hand painted, and others probably from the discount store. They were also different sizes, ranging from as tiny as a thimble to as large as a soccer ball.

Everyone in town knew Mrs. Carter loved cowbells. It began with a small collection of maybe ten. But then, every Christmas, patrons would bring one as a gift to add to the collection. Soon the wooden shelves multiplied and now there was even talk of building an addition just to house cowbells—like a cowbell museum.

"Nice, out-of-the-way spot," Sarah said when she arrived at the table.

"Yeah. We figured being back in the corner they'd let us stay as long as we want," Kat said, flopping back into her chair.

"They'll let you stay all day as long as you keep ordering," Sarah said.

"Sleep well?" Michele asked. "You seemed pretty beat."

Sarah pulled out a chair. "I wish I didn't sleep quite as long."

Theresa leaned over and patted her hand. "It was a tough night and we all thought that you needed the rest. Your body knew when it needed to get up."

"Well…thanks…for… putting me up."

"Of course," the others echoed together.

Then an awkward silence.

Sarah knew they all wanted to ask more, but she wasn't willing to talk. Not yet. Not until she had all the answers figured out for herself.

"Well, well, well. If it isn't little Sarah Cosgrave." Mrs. Carter bustled to the table and gave Sarah a sideways hug. Outside of the grey hair, she hadn't changed much in the past eight years. She moved a little slower than Sarah remembered but still had that ebullient personality that invited every restaurant guest to be part of a bigger family.

"How ya doin'? I heard you was in the hospital and you and Tom Pawlak are now takin' care of those two Davidson boys. It's all such a shame. All that happened in that family is just a shame. How those two boys doin'? They're lucky to have you. Some folks don't take in strays like that, ya know. And you and Tom finally gettin' married too. Now that's good and proper."

Sarah pasted on a smile. "Everyone is managing as best as can be expected under the circumstances."

"That's good. Real good." Mrs. Carter patted her shoulder. "The whole town is looking forward to your weddin'. I haven't been out to your folk's farm since before your mother died. Lookin' forward to it for sure."

Sarah nodded, unwilling to add more gossip to the town loop. "It hasn't changed too much. Just some paint, a new roof, and making sure the house doesn't fall down around us."

"That Tom Pawlak sure took good care of your daddy. I'll bet he's takin' good care of that farm too and those boys. Yep, sure lookin' forward to the wedding."

Mrs. Carter took the order book out of her apron. "You havin' the short stack, honey?"

"That would be great," Sarah said. "But just plain with the butter and syrup on the side."

"Just like your daddy. I guess that's fittin'."

"I have to watch my figure these days." Sarah said. "I'm not getting any younger."

Mrs. Carter chuckled. "You are younger than my grandchildren, missy. No need to worry about that figure. Though I guess every bride is watchin' her figure before her weddin' day. One short stack, everything on the side coming up."

She turned to leave, then stopped mid stride and turned back toward their table. "I like your friends there too," she said, waving a hand in their direction. "Fine ladies. They come in here almost every day and they tip good like proper folk." Then she hurried away and disappeared behind the swinging doors.

Every time someone mentioned the wedding, Sarah felt a little sick to her stomach.

"What's wrong, Sarah?" Michele asked. "You look like someone just trampled on your heart."

"Do I?" Sarah scanned her friend's faces. "I'm just…" Did she really want to talk about this?

"You're not having second thoughts are you?" Theresa said. "I know you and the boys are going through a rough patch but it will work out. They've just been through a lot and need some space."

"I know," Sarah said. "I'm just not sure it's best for all of us to be a family."

"Say what?" Kat burst out. "You and Tom are madly in love. The boys adore you. You two are like the best love story on the Hallmark channel. Hunky hero shows his vulnerable side by taking care of mean Dad, saves heroine from evil witch, and does it all while caring for two small orphaned boys. Oh and the cutest border collie ever. What's wrong with this picture? It always ends in happily-ever-after!"

Even with Kat's penchant for making every relationship into a Hallmark movie moment, Sarah had to admit her summary wasn't too far from reality. On the surface it all looked miraculous.

"I know we promised not to pry," Theresa said. "But being as you brought it up, we are all worried about you. Are you really talking about calling off the wedding? Is there something you aren't telling us? Something Tom did that has made it all go sour?"

"No! Tom is perfect." The last thing she wanted to do was lay any blame on Tom. "None of this is his fault. That's the problem. I just can't fix all of this. As long as I'm a part of this new family, I pose a risk to everyone. Amanda will never let us live together in peace. She will always be between us. She will always want revenge and it will ruin whatever sense of good the boys have managed to eke out of their previous family. I can't let that happen. The only way to save everyone is to walk away."

"Hold on there," Rachel spoke up. "I know I'm not the most together person. But one of the things I learned in therapy is that you can't let evil control your actions for the rest of your life."

"I'm not," Sarah said. "Amanda doesn't control me. That's why I choose to leave."

"Wrong, kiddo," Rachel said. "First place, Amanda is locked up forever. Two life sentences served back to back means she is never getting out of prison."

"I know but—"

Rachel held up a finger. "Hold on. I'm still doing the big sister thing here. Second, how do you think that leaving this family is saving anyone? If anything, it will cause more pain because now that the boys have fallen in love with you and Tom, after they've put their trust in your love, you are going to just walk out of their life? How does that make any sense?"

Sarah worried her bottom lip. She'd thought of what kind of an impact calling off the wedding might have. But in the end she felt called to make the sacrifice for the good of everyone.

"I hear what you're saying," Sarah acknowledged. "But I believe I'm doing what's best for everyone. The boys have bonded with Tom, not me. And it's all so confusing for them. They need someone to blame for everything that has happened to their family, and I'm willing to take that blame so they can be whole again."

Michele reached over and covered Sarah's hand. She said in her quiet voice, "I know you think that sacrificing yourself is the honorable thing to do. But have you considered that you can't make this decision for everyone in your family? Don't they have a say in this?"

"I…I don't know what you mean," Sarah said.

"Do you remember when David and I had that big row while we were on tour, and when the RV broke down and we were too broke to get it fixed? David said he would pay for it, and I refused to let him do that. Even when he offered it as a loan I still refused—for all of us."

Sarah nodded. Everyone but Michele thought she was being selfish not to let David help with the repair. In fact, after several days, they'd all voted and overrode Michele's decision even if it meant she had to leave the band.

"We were a family," Michele continued. "But I was making the decision for all of us without taking your needs into consideration. Is that what you are doing too, Sarah? Are you forgetting that Tom and Connor and Grady should be part of this too?"

"But it's not the same," Sarah said. "We were all adults so we should have had a say. In my situation, Connor and Grady are too young to make this decision. They don't know what life with me and Tom will be like. And they will always have Tom as their constant. Tom is an amazing father to them. He will make sure they are well taken care of. And, eventually, he will find someone who has no past with him or Amanda and he can get married in peace without dealing with all the baggage I bring to the relationship."

"And what about Tom's choice in this decision," Michele pushed. "Does he have a say?"

"Well…no," Sarah said, realizing it sounded like she was contradicting her own logic. "Tom loves me so he can't be clear-headed about this. But I can. I must. It's because I love them so much that I have to be the one to make the sacrifice. I have to be the one to give them a chance at a better life than they can have with me."

"But you don't know their life will be better without you," Kat said. "For all you know it may be amazing. It may be you are the best mother those boys could ever have *because* of your past with their mom."

Sarah wished what Kat said was true, but she just couldn't take the chance. She was afraid this mistake was only the first of many. She'd seen that sometimes love just wasn't enough.

"Oh, honey." Theresa hugged her tight. "I think you better pray on this. I don't think God is calling you to sacrifice yourself or the love you have for Tom and those boys on a possible better future without you. I think you've let Amanda get inside your head. It's understandable with all you've been through."

"But I *have* been praying on this and I'm not hearing an answer," Sarah said.

"Maybe it's the question, sweetie," Theresa said. "Are you asking for a sign to show you the right path and promise success? Or are you asking for help in trusting God to provide for you and your family?"

Sarah had no response. She wasn't sure. Perhaps her own faith wasn't as strong as she thought. Did she expect guarantees or did she trust God would be there in times of trouble? She'd heard many sermons on prayer and she'd been sure she knew all about it.

"Please promise me you won't do anything rash," Theresa continued. "Please continue to pray on this. Don't run away from this open door."

"I'm not running away," Sarah insisted. "I admit, when I left Broken Bow as an eighteen-year-old, I was running away. But not this time. This time I'm...I'm..."

She was beginning to have doubts. But were those doubts only because she wanted it all to work, even though it couldn't? Or was it God asking her to trust in Him? It felt as if a heavy weight had been lifted from her chest, but replaced by a vice. It hurt, but in a different way.

"I promise I'll pray on it," she finally said.

CHAPTER 8

Tom dragged himself around the maze one last time after the last guest exited, just in case someone was still in there. When he got to the center he worked his way back, turning off each hidden flashlight along the way. Next, he walked over to the barn and checked on the animals before closing it up. It wouldn't have been a surprise to find a couple of teens making out in a corner. He could remember doing that himself when he was in high school...with Sarah.

On the way back to the house he poured sand and then water on the open campfire closer to the house where the Rogers had cooked hot dogs and hamburgers on a grill over open flame. He settled into one of the Adirondack chairs around the campfire circle and scanned the property while he waited to make sure there would be no flame left when he went into bed.

He'd sent Grady to bed about nine o'clock when one of the guests said a little boy was asleep on a hay bail at the center and no parent in sight. Grady's job had been to hand out candy to anyone who made it through the maze to the center. Then he'd show them the secret way out a hidden side gate.

Though Connor tried to stay up to midnight when they closed, he was falling off his feet by eleven. Tom found him leaning against the barn with his eyes closed. He didn't even rouse when Tom called his name. Tom had carried him into the house, removed his shoes and jacket and laid him on the sofa with an afghan until he could get back to the house at the end of the night.

The past week without Sarah had taken a toll on all of them. Grady had settled back into family life as if nothing had happened. He did ask about Sarah once today. He wondered if she would come to the maze. When Tom said no, Grady's reaction was neutral. It was just acceptance.

Connor never asked about Sarah. Instead he buried himself in chores around the farm. He'd come straight home from school and then immediately go do his chores. He never complained, never asked questions, and only spoke when asked a direct question. Tom supposed Grady and Connor didn't talk about Sarah because Tom didn't. He just didn't know what to say. He didn't want to make any promises he couldn't keep, so he avoided saying anything.

Had he been wrong to ask her to leave her own home so Grady would agree to return? In hindsight, maybe he should have stood up to Grady and insisted they all work this out together. What kind of parent lets a four-year-old dictate terms for the entire family? Certainly not a good parent.

Did he let Sarah take the brunt of this because he was angry with her for taking the call from Amanda? He ran his hand over the top of his head. Maybe not consciously, but he didn't try hard enough to stop her from leaving either.

How could he be angry with Sarah after all she'd been through? He'd just lost it. The score was Amanda two, Sarah and Tom zero. Even with Amanda in prison, it seemed she still had power over their lives. How long would her power last?

He shook his head in denial. She would be a part of them forever—not just in what she did to him or to Sarah, but because she was Grady and Connor's mother. Even though she'd never get out of prison in her lifetime, they would always be dealing with her in their memories. They would always be comparing themselves to her.

Tom knew it first hand. It was how he'd felt about his abusive father. Growing up he'd always worried he would become like that—like it was in his DNA and something he couldn't control. He'd eventually realized he had a choice, but that wasn't until well into his twenties.

He kicked more dirt into the fire and then headed into the house. He showered and fell into bed. The clock said 1:30. Later this morning, he said to himself. He'd call Sarah in the morning after Connor caught the bus for school. And Grady? He'd find a way to deal with Grady.

A week seemed like forever. As each day passed, it seemed like the open door to her heart was getting smaller. The question was how long until she closed it for good.

Tom checked on Grady. He was in front of the television watching Wild Kratts—part cartoon and part real actors. A pair of zoologist brothers found themselves in crazy situations where they end up parsing out cool facts about animals. It was Grady's favorite show.

He went to Sarah's bedroom and closed the door. He stacked the pillows and propped himself on the bed. He'd taken to sleeping here since she left. Partly for more space away from the boys, and partly because he felt closer to her here. He took a deep breath and dialed her cell.

"Hello." Sarah sounded hesitant.

"How are things at the hotel?"

"Everything's fine. We've all settled in well."

"Is this a good time to talk?" he asked.

He heard a deep sigh. "As good as any I guess," she said.

"Good. I've missed you."

"Me too," she said softly.

"I have to apologize. I shouldn't have sent you away. I should have found a way to handle everything with Grady. I should have picked him up and brought him home and have us all work together through the problem...as a family. I handled it all wrong."

"No, you did the right thing," Sarah said. "The children must come first. I understand. How is Grady doing now?"

"I think he's okay. He seems happy to be home."

"Has he asked about me?"

"Actually, he asked about you last night. He wondered why you didn't come to the maze."

"Oh...I forgot all about it. It seems like ages ago you drew the picture and planned it out."

"Less than a month ago. But I know what you mean."

"How's Connor?" she asked. "He seems so mature for his age. He's had too much to handle. You're still taking him to his counselor, right?"

"Yes. His next appointment is tomorrow. I think it helps a lot. Thank you for that. I would have never thought of it. Counseling was never a part of my life growing up."

"Mine either," Sarah admitted. "But I've trusted it ever since Rachel did six months of therapy after her rape. Before it, I was certain she was going to die."

"Have you thought about a counselor for yourself?" Tom knew Sarah was all about being strong and independent, but seeing how it helped Connor helped him believe Sarah could benefit too.

He waited in the silence.

"I talked to someone once or twice in the hospital," she said. "But I don't really need any help. I mean...I need to learn how to deal with people better. But that's on me, not on anything that happened to me."

HE DECIDED NOT to push further. The last thing he wanted was for her to run or to think he was being judgmental.

"Speaking of apologies...I..." Her voice caught and he thought he detected tears. "I'm truly sorry about all the mistakes I made...taking Amanda's call. I should have listened to you."

"It wasn't just you," he soothed. "It was me too. I just didn't trust her. I've never trusted her since I left her after high school."

"I should have listened to you," Sarah repeated. "I know you'll never forgive me, but—"

"Hold on a minute. I forgave you before you left the house. I never expected you to stay away a whole week. I thought a day, maybe two at the most."

"I thought I could save her." Sarah choked on the words. "I always rush in to save people, even if they don't want to be saved." Her voice was now barely a whisper as if she were talking to herself. "I tried to save you in high school, and we know how that turned out. I tried to save daddy, but he didn't want to be saved either."

Tom heard the tears in her voice. "Sarah…please…"

"Why can't I learn that lesson?" She begged as she sobbed. "I was so stupid to choose trying to save Amanda over you and the boys."

"Sarah, you are not stupid." His voice rose in alarm. "Don't ever say that about yourself. We've both made choices we regret. Mine was allowing Amanda into our lives in the first place. Then I compounded it by not being forceful in turning down her advances."

Tom wished he could go back in time. He'd forgiven himself for all that happened when he was a teenager. But he wanted to start over and reject Amanda the first time she came on to him after her marriage. He knew she was bad news, but he'd tried to be kind in his rejections or to make a joke of it. That had been a big mistake. He didn't become forceful with Amanda until she tried to come onto him in Sarah's presence, right here on the farm.

"You can't help her, Sarah. Her obsession is an illness. An illness that I don't know can ever be cured. That's why she's in prison. She can't stop herself."

"I know that now." Her voice quivered and Tom wished he could reach through the phone lines and wrap her in his arms.

"I want you to come home," he finally said. "You need to be here. With us. Connor and Grady miss you. I miss you. Come home and let us be a family again. We are stronger together."

"I…I can't." She said.

"What are you saying, Sarah? You can't now or you can't ever?"

"I don't know. I don't know that I'm the right one for you and the boys. I don't know that I can ever be the right one."

"You are the right one! You have been the best thing that ever happened to me and to the Grady and Connor."

"I don't know," she said again. "There's too much in our past now. I can't heal the rupture. I thought I could but I don't have the power."

Tom held his breath and felt the immediate loss of air in his lungs. He consciously told himself to breathe again.

"I don't understand. We love you. *I* love you. We can work this out. Don't give up on us now—now that you've worked so hard to put Amanda behind you. Behind all of us."

He realized that he'd been letting Sarah do most of the parenting since she'd come home. She always seemed to know the right thing to say, the right thing to do. She had been the one to work so hard to integrate this family and to make sure the boys felt safe—even when she was in the hospital she was thinking of them. She'd been the one to make it easy for Tom to keep working the farm while she kept the house together—cooking and cleaning.

She was the one who helped Connor with his homework after school while Tom was still working in the field mending fences, or watering crops, or fixing the barn. Sarah was the one who planned educational field trips for Grady. Sometimes she watched the Wild Kratts with him and then let him shine as he recounted amazing facts he'd learned about the animals. She'd always been the one to listen to the boys—their fears and concerns—and to make sure they were being heard.

"Please, Sarah. Give us one more chance to make this right."

"I'm trying," she said after a long pause. "I'm trying to make the right decision for all of us."

"Come for a visit then. Let's talk about it together. You don't have to stay. Talk to the boys. Let them have a say. At least let you and I have some time together."

"I don't think I can do that," she said, her voice shaking once again. "If I see you again, I won't have the will power to leave."

"You've already decided to leave then? No wedding?"

"Yes...I mean no. I don't know. I...I promised Theresa I would pray about it. And I have been, but it's not working. I don't know what else to do."

His stomach dropped and he squeezed his eyes shut to absorb the pain of her leaving. He curled into the phone, holding it tight to his head with both hands as if it was the only thing he had left to keep them together.

"I love you, Tom. And I love the boys. I really wanted this but... I just...I just..."

Through the haze of her voice he realized he had no power to change her mind. For once he had to be the one to step into faith. He had to be the one to give up control and believe.

"I'll put my faith in you and God," he whispered it like a prayer. "If you say you are praying on it. Truly praying. Then I trust you will find the right answer."

"But you don't believe." Sarah's quiet voice seemed to beg him to affirm his faith.

"I don't know what I believe," he admitted. "I believe in God. I just don't know why He would choose to intervene in my life. All I know is I've done everything I can to get you to stay and it hasn't worked. I have to start somewhere. I may not believe in the way you do. But I trust *you*. And maybe that is part of God's plan. If we can't trust each other..."

His breath caught. He couldn't finish the thought. He wasn't ready to let go of the belief they could still be together—that they would still be married on Thanksgiving Day.

"Tom?"

He let out the breath. "Still here."

"I'm so sorry," she said.

"Listen Sarah, do what you need to do. I know you well enough that I know you give up your will to God when you pray. I've never been able to do that—to truly give up control in that way. But I love who you are. I love everything about you. Your faith is at the core of who you have become. I know your prayers *will* lead you in the right path for you. I pray that path brings you back to me and the boys."

"Thank you," she whispered.

"Make no mistake. Unless you tell me otherwise, I will be standing right here on our porch, dressed in my Sunday finest on Thanksgiving day, ready to marry you. I love you, Sarah. I want to spend the rest of my life with you. When you pray, be sure to tell God that. Be sure He knows what is at stake at here. Then open yourself to His will."

"He knows," she said.

"I believe that too," Tom admitted.

Neither one spoke for quite some time.

"I love you, Tom."

"I know."

"Thank you for believing. That means more to me than you can know."

He heard the click as she hung up.

I do believe, he said to himself. It's trusting in that belief that's the problem.

He slowly removed the phone from his ear and uncurled on Sarah's bed. He moved in a haze down the hall and into the living room. Though it seemed like hours they were on the phone, Grady was still immersed in watching the Kratts. He checked his watch. Less than half an hour had passed. In less than half an hour he may have lost the love of his life…again.

He quietly opened and closed the screen door and stepped onto the front porch. The trees were at their peak fall colors. Some had completed the change and brown leaves were dropping daily—covering everything. Others were still holding tight to their bright yellows or reds, and even some deep purples.

Tom looked up to the bright blue sky. Today there wasn't a single cloud. He knew that some believed the order found in the universe was proof of the existence of God. But if God did create the universe, why would he care about the affairs of man? Humans wee but a spec in the universe. That had always been the sticking point for Tom. He closed his eyes to the bright sun.

I don't know if you're up there in the sky, God. Or if you're here on earth as some kind of ethereal presence. I don't know if you live in the hearts of good men or if that is only a way for us to feel like we have control over our lives. But Sarah believes in you with all of her being, and I want to believe too. So, I'm putting my faith in you. She can't carry this burden alone, and she won't let me carry it with her. I'm asking you to provide a path for this family—a path that will be the best for all four of us and provide a good foundation for the challenges ahead. Thy will be done. Amen.

When Tom finished his prayer, he felt as if a heavy burden had been lifted from his shoulders. He still had no answers, but he no longer felt completely alone.

CHAPTER 9

Connor was up early on Saturday, determined to get all his chores done before breakfast. It was only five days until Thanksgiving and there wasn't any news about the wedding. Last night, Daddy sat him and Grady down and explained that the wedding might not happen. That Miss Sarah, their new mommy, might need more time.

Connor had been thinking hard every day since Miss Sarah left when Grady ran away. He knew she was scared and didn't know what to do. He even talked to his counselor about it. After the talk, he figured his daddy didn't know what to do either, so it was up to him.

All night he went over his plan again and again. It had to work. He had to save his family. But it all depended on Grady agreeing to it. And Miss Kat. She had to agree to help because Grady was too little to do his part alone. And his counselor told him that Connor was always the conductor of his train. That meant it was up to him to conduct the train so it didn't run off the tracks.

He'd secretly called the hotel yesterday before he left for school, when Daddy was harvesting the garden early in the morning. He knew Miss Kat was the only one who could help 'cause she wasn't too old yet. Her brain wasn't too affected with adult stuff. She was pretty old—almost eighteen. But she wasn't nearly as old as everyone else and she immediately understood the problem. She said she'd been thinking on it too.

Once he explained his plan, she'd agreed to meet him and Grady today and discuss it. She said there were a few things they needed to change to really make it work right.

Connor finished his chores in the barn, and then ran toward the porch to go get Grady and get his secret plan in place. He stopped short when he saw Daddy sitting in the porch chair near the door. The heat rose from his coffee cup and he slowly took a sip, his eyes peering over the edge at Connor.

"You're up early," Daddy said with his rough morning voice. It always took a couple of cups before Daddy sounded normal. "Everything okay?"

Connor leaned on the stair post, one hip canted out. It was important to be casual. He couldn't tell Daddy about his secret plan. He might try to stop him.

"Yep," he said. "Just wanted to get done early."

"You mucked out the stalls?"

"Yes, sir."

"Put in fresh water, got the horses their oats?"

"Yes, sir."

"Checked the hay?"

"Yes. It's all done."

"You're a good boy." Daddy leaned back in the chair. "So what's your plan?"

Connor's eyes opened wide and he stood straight, a big ball of spit formed on his tongue and he had to swallow. How could Daddy know he had a plan? He hadn't said anything. This was a secret plan. He couldn't know. Could he read his mind?"

"Um…is Grady up yet?" Connor asked quickly.

"Yep. He's finishing his breakfast, then he'll be out."

"Good," Connor said.

"You and Grady have a plan for today? I'm going to be doing some patchwork on the barn roof most of the morning. After lunch, I'd like you and Grady to help me finish picking the vegetables in the garden. You have some schoolwork to do this morning? Or some games you can play with Grady?"

Connor relaxed a little. Daddy didn't know about the plan after all. "No school work. I was thinking Grady and I could go inspect fences. I was thinkin' I could teach him how to look for holes and stuff. We could mark it with that orange paint stick so it's easy for you to find and fix 'em later."

"Hmmm." Daddy scrunched up his eyes and looked at Connor like maybe he was suspicious. "Sounds more like adventurin' to me."

Connor scuffed his boot in the ground. "Grady does like adventurin' but we could do both at the same time."

Daddy smiled. "Sounds like a good plan. I used to like adventuring when I was your age too. Always made the weekends go fast. Fall is the best time of year for adventuring, with all the colors changing on the trees, and the fields hanging on to the last grass before winter. You have your watch on?"

"Yes, sir." Connor pointed to it on his wrist. "It says eight-oh-four."

"You be sure to be back at the house by noon. That gives you almost four hours of adventuring and fence marking. But you have to promise me you will not go outside the fence and you will keep Grady with you at all times."

"I promise." Connor made a cross on his heart.

Daddy stood and mussed the hair on top Connor's head. "You're a good boy. You two have fun this morning. Don't forget, be back here at noon. Don't be late."

Connor threw his arms around Daddy's waist. "I love you, Daddy. You know that, right?"

Daddy dropped to one knee and hugged him back. "What's this about, Connor? You know I will always love you no matter what."

Connor was counting on the no-matter-what part once his plan got going.

"Is everything okay?" Daddy asked as he let go. "Anything you want to talk about?"

Connor shook his head.

"You sure?"

No, he wasn't sure. He was afraid Daddy was getting suspicious again. "I just miss Mommy," he said. "I mean Miss Sarah-mommy."

"Yeah, I miss her too. You know we've talked about this. She needs some time to figure things out. You don't need to worry about her."

"I know but the wedding is on Thursday and she's not thinking fast enough."

Daddy sighed. "A lot has happened in the last couple months and Miss Sarah is having a crisis of faith."

"What does that mean?" Connor asked. "You said she always has faith."

"She does," Daddy assured him. "But sometimes, even when you have faith, it's hard to see which path to take. Do you remember when you and Grady took a hike with me in the woods at Beavers Bend State Park? And when we were really far away from the car, the rain clouds came in and it got dark all of a sudden?"

"Yeah, Grady started cryin' 'cause we was lost and we didn't think we'd ever get out of there and find our way home. And I was a little scared too," Connor admitted.

"But we did find our way, didn't we?" Daddy said.

"I remember you said we had to have faith that we knew the way even if we couldn't see it clearly."

"That's kind of what is happening to Miss Sarah, right now."

"Is she lost? Should we go look for her like we looked for Grady?"

"It's not that kind of lost," Daddy said. "Sometimes people get lost when things don't go the way they expected, and it makes them rethink their feelings. They get all turned around and don't know which way is up. It's like starting to climb uphill on a mountain trail instead of going downhill toward the river."

Connor thought on that a long time. He didn't really understand how people can be lost if they weren't really lost. And everyone knew if you got lost on a trail you were supposed to go downhill and follow the river. He learned that in Cub Scouts.

He remembered his other dad talked about his mom being lost in her mind when she ran away. He'd said she'd lost her way and strayed from the right path. But he didn't mean it like being lost in the woods. Was that what was happening with Miss Sarah? If it were, his big plan wouldn't work.

"Is she…" Connor didn't want to hear the answer, but he had to know. "Is Miss Sarah having sleepovers?"

Daddy crooked his head to one side. "What do you mean by sleepover?"

"When my other mommy ran away…before she…" He couldn't finish it. He still couldn't bring himself to say she killed his daddy, even if he knew she did. He swallowed down his fear. "She was having sleepovers …you know…with other men because she was mad at Daddy and didn't want to sleep with him anymore."

"Oh, God no." Daddy leaned forward and grasped Connors shoulders hard. "That is *not* what Miss Sarah is doing. I promise you. The only sleepover she is having is with her friends from the band—Theresa and Michele and Kat."

"Are you sure?" Connor asked. "Because I never seen you and Miss Sarah sleep in the same bedroom. So maybe she is mad at you and she needs sleepovers."

"Oh geez." Daddy wiped a hand across his forehead and looked to the porch ceiling. "Sit down for a minute." He pointed to the wooden ottoman.

Connor sat carefully. He could tell the question really bothered Daddy and that meant it must be true but he didn't know how to say it.

"It's different with Miss Sarah," Daddy said. "She's different from your mom. She's…her beliefs…" He hesitated and Connor worried even more. "I can't explain everything exactly, but we had an agreement that we wouldn't share the same bedroom until we were married. But we still love each other very much. She just wanted to wait so it would be something special for after we were married. It's kind of like when you promise not to open your Christmas presents until Christmas day. You really want to but waiting makes it even more exciting. Does that make sense?"

Connor nodded, but the truth was he didn't see how sleeping in the same bedroom was like opening Christmas presents. He and Grady shared the same bedroom even when they were mad at each other. He didn't think that waiting to go to bed with Grady was as exciting as opening Christmas presents.

Maybe Daddy didn't really know what was going on. Maybe he just didn't want to see it, like his other daddy didn't want to see it. He just pretended it wasn't happening and never talked about it until it was too late.

"When our other mommy had sleepovers she stopped loving us," Connor finally said. "When she went to live with those other men, she didn't want us anymore because she said those other men didn't want children." He paused to get his thoughts together before continuing. "I think that's why Miss Sarah doesn't want to see us anymore. And we have to find her and make her stop. You have to find her and tell her you love her. And you have to kiss her every day like you did before when she was so happy. And then we can all get married."

Connor stopped to see if Daddy understood what he was saying. He was looking confused. His mouth was open but it seemed stuck 'cause he wasn't saying anything.

"If we don't all get married soon, then Miss Sarah will never be our mommy. And that means she will have to find another family and she will move away and then she can't love us anymore because it's too hard to love two families…and then…"

Connor wiped at his face. He didn't mean to cry. He'd just been holding so much inside for the past month that he couldn't help it. This was why he had to make a plan. They couldn't let Miss Sarah stop loving them. He couldn't take losing two mommies.

Daddy's eyes got a little watery and he gathered Connor into his lap. Connor held tight. He knew he was a little big to still be sitting in Daddy's lap but he didn't care right now. He just wanted someone to make everything right.

"Miss Sarah loves you and Grady more than anything in the whole world," Daddy said. "Believe me. No matter what she decides she will always love you forever and ever. She only wants the very best for you. That's why she's thinking so hard."

"If she loves us then why hasn't she come home?" Connor asked between his tears.

Daddy let out a big breath and rubbed circles on Connor's back. "It's complicated. I don't know if I can explain it."

Connor waited for him to figure it out but Daddy just kept silent. He worried on it until he knew the answer. Oh poor Daddy. Why didn't he think of that before? He sat up and covered his mouth with a hand. "I think I understand. Did she stop loving you, Daddy? Is that why we can't get married? I'm sorry. I was being so selfish, I didn't think of your feelings."

"No," Daddy said. "No, that's not it. She loves me very much. I know it sounds confusing. The problem is she loves all of us even more than she loves herself."

Connor tried to work that around in his head. It didn't make any sense at all. If people really loved each other then they should be together. It was simple. He loved Grady and he stayed with him even when he was being stupid. Sometimes he got mad at him, but they always worked it out. He'd never figure out adults. Whenever they couldn't explain something they always said it was complicated.

He vowed to himself that he would never become an adult because something bad must happen to their brain to make life so complicated. He didn't want complicated anymore.

He climbed out of Daddy's lap and stood tall. He was going to fix this for everybody. If the adults couldn't figure it out, it was up to him and Grady to make sure this wedding happened. If Daddy didn't know how to fix Miss Sarah, he knew even more than ever that his plan had to work.

"I'm going to get Grady now," he said. He made a show of looking at his watch. "We have to get to adventurin' or we won't have enough time."

Daddy looked at him kind of funny. Then he said, "Okay, you boys have fun. Don't forget. Keep Grady near you all the time. Don't let him get too far from you."

"I won't," Connor said as he moved toward the front door.

"And don't forget the red marking paint for the fence holes."

"Yes, sir." Connor rushed into the house before he lost his nerve and gave up the whole plan. The quicker he got Grady out the door, the quicker they could put the plan in place and the quicker they could all get married.

~

"How long are we walkin'?" Grady asked as he fell behind again.

"Just a little bit more," Connor assured him. "I have an important secret to tell you, and Daddy can't hear it."

"He can't hear us already. We've been walkin' forever!" Grady stopped and refused to budge.

"If you don't keep up with me I won't tell you the secret." Connor turned to face Grady. "It's really important. It has to do with the wedding."

Grady ran to catch up. "The wedding? Like a big, big secret?"

"Yep. Bigger than ever," Connor promised. "And you and me and Miss Kat are the only ones who will know it. And it means a big adventure."

"Are we going to meet Miss Kat? Is she going to help us make Miss Sarah come back and be our mommy?"

"I hope so," Connor said. "If this doesn't work, nothing will."

"But Daddy said we had to leave this alone. He said we have to have faith things will turn out," Grady said. "What does that mean? Have faith."

"I don't know for sure. I think faith means believe. Or God will help you. Or, if you believe then God will help you. Something like that. But when our other mommy ran away, Daddy always said God helps those who help themselves. I think that means people still have to do stuff too, not just wait around. And that is what we're doing. We're going to have faith, but we're going to do stuff to help everyone."

Connor angled off to the right toward the farthest corner of the property. He pointed to the big oak tree in the corner. "See that big tree? That's the secret tree that's going to help us. If you can walk just a little farther, then we can sit in the secret tree and I'll tell you the plan."

"Look!" Grady yelled as he took off in a run. "There's Miss Kat!"

Connor ran after him. Miss Kat was waving from the first branch in the tree. She'd come as she said she would. Now he truly believed his plan would work.

CHAPTER 10

Tom waited on the porch for the sun to set over the barn. It was Tuesday and he'd still heard nothing from Sarah.

School was closed all week. Monday and Tuesday were scheduled teacher in-service days; Thursday and Friday were the Thanksgiving holidays. With only one scheduled school day, the district decided to close for the whole week. Tom tried to be upbeat as the boys talked about the wedding and how they could help get everything ready.

Tom didn't know if it was better to disappoint them now and deal with the pain, or let them maintain hope until Thursday morning and disappoint them then. Neither answer had a good outcome.

He never thought Sarah could be this cruel. Surely she knew that losing her would be even worse for the boys than losing Amanda. As cruel as she was, at least Amanda was straight with them. When she left Henry, she told the boys she was leaving and wouldn't be back. She told them not to expect anything. It hurt like hell, but they knew —at least Connor knew—that she made a choice. There was no hoping or guessing and Amanda had withdrawn her love from them a long time before that. Henry had been the real parent.

But with Sarah, they trusted her almost immediately. They bonded with her and made her the new mommy very quickly. She'd always been there for them. They'd leaned on her and never questioned her love. Except for Sunday, when Connor expressed his doubts, both Connor and Grady still had faith that Sarah would follow through—that she'd show up on Thursday and get married.

Tom didn't know what changed Connor's mind. It was as if simply unburdening himself made Connor believe in Sarah again. The next day, it was like he'd never questioned her faithfulness at all.

He swiped his phone on and pressed Sarah's contact number. He was not going to be patient any longer. If she didn't have her answer, then she had to make a decision. That was what adults did.

A week ago, hope had given way to doubt. With each day that passed without talking to her the doubt grew like poison ivy, choking out any belief that she would talk to him again. He'd give her one more chance to come to her senses—one more chance to prove his trust was not in vain, that she was the strong woman of faith he knew and loved.

"Hello, Tom." Kat's voice answered the phone like she had every night for the past week.

"Is Sarah there?" His voice growled with the anger building inside.

"I'm sorry," Kat said. "You know she won't talk to you. She thinks it's easier this way."

"For who?" He asked, struggling against the growing feeling of suffocation. "Her? Or me? Or the boys?"

"I don't know what to say," Kat said.

He didn't want to take his anger out on Kat. Who would let everyone know not to come here on Thursday? He didn't think he could do it himself. He had two little boys to take care of—boys who would be grieving the loss. He had to keep it together. He couldn't continue to take these punches to his heart. And he definitely wouldn't let her do it to Grady and Connor too.

"I know it's hard," Kat said into his silence. "Please don't give up. I still have faith it will work out. We still have tomorrow. Please Tom, hang on for one more day. Just have faith for one more day."

"I can't," he said. "I can't keep the boys hanging. It's too cruel to keep their hopes up. I'm not going to let them be standing on the porch on Thursday and have Sarah never show.

Silence on the line. He knew Kat had no answers for him. No one did but Sarah, and she wasn't talking.

"Tell Sarah something for me," Tom said.

"Yes?"

"Tell her I wish her well, but she needs to get as far away from Broken Bow as possible and never come back. I won't go through this ever again." He stopped to gather himself. He was not going to cry. He had vowed to hold it together no matter what happened.

"You don't mean that, Tom," Kat said. "Please don't give up now when we're so close. Just one more day. Hold tight to faith just one more day. I just know it will work out. It has to work out."

"I can't," he said and hung up the phone.

His heart trembled in fear there would never be a safe harbor for love again. He could feel each beat of his heart against its constricting cage. With every rejection of his calls this week, his heart bruised and swelled until it could no longer be confined.

When he thought he'd lose it and shout at the heavens like a madman, adrenaline spiked and smashed the constricting cage into a hundred angry pieces.

Faith! His mind spat out the word as if it was profanity. Not once in his life did faith help him with anything. It was a word people pulled out of a magician's hat to assuage the fears of children. It was something handy to say when you could not accept responsibility for your own actions.

Faith wasn't enough to cauterize the wounds of two small boys who'd already suffered a lifetime of evil and were growing up too fast. Faith wasn't going to provide them with a new mother when Sarah decided to sacrifice herself on Amanda's altar. Faith wasn't going to give him an instruction guide for how to be a single parent the rest of his life.

Faith would never heal his broken heart.

He let the anger swirl inside him and offer a temporary reprieve from the grief he knew would eventually consume him. Anger could hold him together enough to get through the next two days. He couldn't afford to let grief rip him apart when he needed all his strength to steadfastly hold open the door to sanctuary for two little boys.

~

TOM FELT someone shaking him and he growled. He was stiff from sleeping on the couch last night. He'd locked Sarah's bedroom so he wouldn't be tempted to tear it up.

"Daddy, wake up. Wake up."

He opened his eyes and looked at Connor in his pajamas standing on the porch.

Tom moaned as he sat up. How long had he slept? "What time is it?"

"I don't know. After midnight I think. You have to help. Grady ran away again."

Tom came instantly alert. "What? When? Why?"

"I don't know, I woke up to go to the bathroom and he wasn't in his bed. I already looked all around the house and I can't find him."

"Did you two have a fight?"

"No!"

Tom tried to think back. Was it possible he overheard something in his conversation with Kat? Last time Grady ran away he was angry and hurt.

"We have to find him, Daddy." Connor pulled at Tom's arm.

"Get dressed," Tom ordered. "Hurry."

While Connor dressed he called the Rogers family first. But they said Grady had not shown up there. They promised to search the property though.

Next he thought he'd call Kat. Only he didn't know what her phone number was. He only knew she answered Sarah's phone. Theresa. Did he have Theresa's phone number? He scrolled through his contacts and finally found it and pressed the button."

"Tom, thank God. We are almost to your place. Did you find Grady?"

"What? How do you know he's missing?"

"Kat phoned Sarah at eleven and woke us both up. She said she took the car because she had to find Grady. Then she hung up. About five minutes ago she called back and said she knew where to look—something about a tree on your property. You would know which one. She said Sarah had to come right away and help."

He heard the gravel crunch beneath tires on the driveway and Theresa's car pulled in, headlights on bright. Theresa, Michele, Rachel, and Sarah all poured out of the car.

Sarah reached him first. "I'm so sorry. I'm so sorry I've caused Grady to run away again."

"What do you mean you caused this? You aren't making sense. No one is making sense right now," Tom said.

"Kat said something about an oak tree," Sarah continued. "Where would that be? This is all my fault because I couldn't face myself. I couldn't face you. I couldn't face all the mistakes I would make in the future."

Tom wasn't sure what Sarah was saying. He could barely process anything that was happening. It was like he was caught in a nightmare where everyone was speaking a different language and he was expected to put it all together.

Then all the women started talking at once. He couldn't make out any particular question, and no one seemed to have the story straight from Kat.

Just then Connor came back in his work jeans and a shirt and boots.

"Everyone shut the hell up," Tom yelled.

Connor cowered next to Theresa.

"Something is not right," he said, his voice controlled again. "Connor, what's going on? What do you know about this?"

Connor stood perfectly still, frozen like a deer caught in the headlights.

"Did you call Kat tonight to tell her Grady had runaway? Did you call her before you woke me up?"

Connor's face turned ashen. "I…um…yes…kind of."

"Step out here where I can see you." Tom pointed to a spot right in front of him. "I'm not going to hurt you. I just want the truth."

Connor stepped in front of Tom, his back straight as a soldier ready to march to the battlefield.

Tom knelt on one knee to be at eye level with Connor. "Why did you call Kat before talking to me?"

"Don't be mad," Connor said, his voice shaking just a little. "Someone had to do something."

"What do you mean?" Tom asked. "Who had to do what."

Connor tugged at Tom's hand. "Please, I know where he is. You have to go there. Please, we have to hurry. He's way far up in the tree and he can't get down on his own."

"Where are we going? How do you know he's in a tree?" Tom asked as he stood again.

Connor tugged his hand again. "Everyone can come. Everyone can help."

Tom knew deep inside something was very wrong with this scenario, but he also knew it was important to Connor to play this out. He just hoped that Connor hadn't put Grady in any real danger.

"Any of you have a flashlight with you?" Tom asked the group.

All three women tapped their cell phones and turned them into flashlights.

Tom scanned their shoes. Thank goodness no one had chosen to wear heels. Theresa and Rachel wore tennis shoes, while Michele and Sarah wore boots.

"I warned them about the ground," Sarah said.

Tom stepped in front of everyone and then motioned to Connor. "Lead the way."

He made sure to keep several steps ahead of Sarah. He knew he couldn't watch her walk from behind. He couldn't afford to let any feelings get in his way again. In fact, he wished she hadn't come. It just made everything that much more difficult. If Grady had heard some part of his conversation with Kat and that upset him, he was afraid that Sarah's presence would make things even worse.

Nothing to do about it now, he told himself as they all trudged toward some unknown tree. An oak tree? If he weren't so scared for Grady, he would have laughed. There were probably a hundred different oak trees on this property. If Connor knew where this particular oak tree was, then he'd surely planned this whole thing.

After twenty minutes of walking, Connor pointed to the furthest northwest corner of the property. "That's where Grady is. He climbed up really far."

Kat was on the ground, looking up.

Sarah ran ahead. "Grady, where are you?" she shouted when she reached Kat at the base.

"He's been asking for you," Kat said. "He said he won't come down until you and Mr. Tom talk to him."

"Boost me," Sarah said to Kat.

Tom stepped in and stood as close to Sarah as he had in three weeks. "I'll do it. I'll follow behind to make sure you don't fall."

He held his hands together in a cup at about knee height and she placed her foot firmly into it. He lifted her up and she grasped the lowest branch and started climbing slowly. "I'm coming, Grady," she said as she climbed. "Don't move. I'm coming to you."

Tom jumped and grabbed the first branch on his own after she'd moved a few feet up. He pulled his body weight up and swung a leg over the first branch, then stood and climbed right behind her. "Hang on tight, Grady," he said. "I'm coming too. We don't want you to fall."

Flashlights from below illuminated the combination of red and yellow leaves in light and shadow. Sarah and Tom climbed in and out of the light. After a few more branches, he saw Grady snuggled into a strong nook. He reached up to help him down. He'd been tied into place with heavy rope lashed around his torso and legs. There was no way he could fall off.

Sarah looked at Tom and tilted her head to one side, looking first at Grady then back at Tom. Then she settled in a branch where she was even with him. "How are you doing, Grady?"

"I'm a little tired," he said.

"I bet you are. Did you tie that rope all by yourself?"

"Um…I forgot," Grady said.

Tom stood on the branch he held instead of sitting. "So, what's this all about?"

"It's about family," Grady said. "It's about you being our mommy and daddy and not being very good at it."

"Who helped you get up here?" Tom asked.

"I'm not 'sposed to say."

"I can guess," Sarah said. "Kat was part of this some how."

"I'm not saying." Grady clamped his lips shut in a show of defiance.

"I know this tree," Sarah said. "I used to climb it all the time when I was a little girl. Especially when I was sad or confused or mad at my daddy."

"Are you mad at me, Grady," Tom asked.

"I'm mad at both of you."

"I don't blame you," Sarah said. "I let you down, didn't I?"

"I don't know what that means," Grady said. "I'm mad because you are both big fat liars."

"Now wait a minute." Tom bristled at that. He'd never told a lie in his life.

"You are," Grady insisted.

Sarah stroked Tom's arm and he held back his retort.

"What did we lie about?" she asked.

"Ask Connor. He can say it better."

Tom knew Connor was in on this. He didn't think Grady would easily agree to come all the way out here on his own in the middle of the night and climb this tree. He certainly didn't tie himself in. Sarah had guessed right on that. Connor and Kat had cooked this up.

"Connor, you better get up here," Tom said. "It seems you are the director here."

"Grady, you promised not to tell," Connor yelled up.

"I couldn't help it," Grady yelled down. "I forgot how to 'splain everything."

Soon Connor joined them. "Darn it, Grady," he said. "We practiced all this."

"I know, but I got confused. I don't know about love stuff. I only know that I love Mommy and Daddy so much I feel like my heart will burst if they don't get married. And then, when I even think about it, I start crying, and then I can't talk and I can't think. And…"

His sobs interrupted his explanation and Tom and Sarah both reached for him at the same time.

"You are explaining just fine," Sarah choked out between her own tears.

"You see," Connor said, his voice also breaking. "How can you really love us when you don't want to live together as a family?"

"It's not that easy," Sarah said. "It's complicated."

"Stop using that word!" Connor raised his voice. "That's the way adults don't answer the questions."

No one spoke for what seemed like forever. Finally Tom couldn't stand it anymore. "You're right, Connor. We don't know all the answers. We try, but we don't know."

"Miss Sarah—Mommy, do you love Daddy or not?" Connor asked.

Sarah looked at Tom and said, "I love him with all my heart."

"Daddy do you really love Mommy?" Connor asked Tom.

He clasped his free hand with hers and looked into her eyes. "I do. I never thought I'd have a second chance with you. All I've ever wanted was to be with you for the rest of my life—even when I was running scared, all I wanted was you."

He paused. Was he really opening his heart to her again? No matter what he told Kat to say to Sarah, his heart could never close to another chance.

"If I did something wrong, I'm sorry," Tom said. "I can't fix it if you don't let me."

"You did nothing wrong," Sarah assured him. "It's me. It's always been me who was the problem."

"Mommy," Connor interrupted them. "You told us that families stay together no matter what. That's what you said when you first came to help Daddy take care of us. That's what you said love is about.

Families work things out even when it's hard, even when they're scared. I don't understand why you're scared because your big and Grady and me are little, and we aren't scared to be a family. But now you want to run away, and Daddy is sad all the time. And he can't explain it either. If you run away we can never be a family and that means you don't really believe what you said."

Tom couldn't speak. Connor had said everything he'd wanted to say to Sarah himself but couldn't.

Sarah looked to Connor and then Grady, her eyes filled with tears. She looked back to Tom. "What a stupid, prideful, self-righteous fool I've been."

"Sarah…"

"No, don't make excuses for me. It's true." She reached out to Connor; her fingers skimmed the side of his jaw. "I'm so sorry I hurt you, Connor, and you too, Grady." She patted her hand against his free arm. "I made a big mistake. I thought I knew what was best. I thought I could design a better path for everyone by stepping away. You are absolutely right. I was scared. I was so scared I couldn't even hear God answering my prayers.

"But he did answer. He answered as he always does, with love. With the innocence of two children he answered with love. With the faithfulness of a good man, he answered with love. I just didn't see it."

"I don't know what you just said," Connor interrupted. "But I think it's good, right?"

Sarah chuckled. "Yes, it's very good. You are right. Families do stay together no matter what. They work things out together. And the most important thing is if they truly love each other they trust each other, and they always talk to each other about what's bothering them. You showed me that today. I love all of you more than anything in the world."

"That's what Daddy said!" Connor smiled.

"You have a smart daddy." Sarah leaned forward and gave Tom a quick kiss.

"Yay!" Grady clapped his hands. "Does this mean we are getting married?"

Sarah laughed. "Yes, we are all getting married. The whole family."

"We're getting married!" Grady shouted as loud as he could down to those at the bottom of the tree.

"Finally!" Kat said loudly. "I knew it would work. I knew it!"

~

TOM STOOD on the porch beaming at the guests sitting on the hay bales in front of him. Connor stood next to him and waved to the Rogers family in the second row. The Sweetwater Canyon women had taken turns serenading the crowd from the back of a truck. They'd switched in and out between tunes to help Sarah get dressed.

All of the Sweetwater Canyon family was now seated in the front row of hay bales. Michele sat with her husband, David, and their two children. Rachel held tight to Noel's hand. His daughter Claire had been playing fiddle moments earlier but was now leaning against her dad. Theresa and Kat took up the seats at the end of the front row. He could see Theresa already had out a hanky, and Kat was patting her mother's hand.

Tom fiddled with his bolo tie. He wore his best non-denim slacks, a crisp white collared shirt and a black vest. He called it his only Sunday-go-to-church outfit. Connor wore the same thing.

The pastor of Sarah's church stepped up next to Tom.

"You ready, son?" he asked.

"I've been waiting for Sarah for it seems like forever," Tom said.

"And you, Connor, are you ready too?"

"Yes sir," Connor responded with the biggest smile Tom had seen in a long time.

The band stopped playing and Sarah appeared on the other side of the pastor holding Grady's hand. Grady was also dressed like Tom. He looked out to the guests and smiled.

"Tom. Sarah." The pastor motioned to a spot directly in front of him. "Will you step here and join hands?"

Tom caressed the side of her hands with his fingers as he breathed in the vision before him. She was absolutely perfect in a simple floor-length white gown with a hint of lace. Her head was crowned with a double band of pearls. He couldn't help but run the edge of his hand over the bangs that peaked out in front of the headband. He remembered when there was no hair on that head and he thought he might lose her forever. He loved her short hair now.

"We are gathered here together," the pastor began, "to celebrate the marriage of Tom Pawlak and Sarah Cosgrave and the union of this new family that includes Grady Davidson and Connor Davidson."

Tom listened to the opening prayer and silently added his own thanks to God for bringing them all together again.

The pastor's remarks spoke of new beginnings, of faith, and trust. He stressed the importance of making faith the center of their marriage.

"Do you, Tom Pawlak, take Sarah Cosgrave to be your wife? Do you promise to love, honor, and cherish her, forsaking all others and hold only unto her?"

Tom held both her hands and looked in her eyes. "I do."

"Do you, Sarah Cosgrave, take Tom Pawlak to be your husband? Do you promise to love, honor, and cherish him, forsaking all others and hold only unto him?"

Sarah's eyes misted, but she held firm. "I do."

After the blessing and exchange of the rings, it was time to include the children.

The pastor said, "Often marriage is viewed as the union of two people. Yet marriages not only unite the couple, they can unite families as well."

He turned to Connor. "Connor, do you wish to be united today with this family taking both Tom and Sarah as your parents?"

Connor stood tall. "I do."

The pastor turned toward Grady and motioned for him to step forward. "Grady, do you wish to be united today with this family taking both Tom and Sarah as your parents?"

Grady stepped forward and smiled broadly. He looked out to the field of people witnessing this event and nodded his head in an exaggerated way. "I finally, definitely do."

Giggles rippled across the yard. Then he stepped back.

"Please take the children's hands and form a circle," the pastor instructed. Tom and Sarah put one child on either side so that both of them held the hand of each child.

"Do you, Tom and Sarah Pawlak, take Grady and Connor Davidson to love, cherish, and protect as your own children until the end of your days?"

They squeezed hands with each other and the boys. "We gladly do."

The pastor guided them toward a group of candles in front of them. "Tom, would you light the four candles in the outside ring?"

Tom nodded and lit each one.

"Light is the essence of our existence. When God gave light to the world, he also created a part of himself to live in each of us. That individual light within each of us represents our hopes, our dreams and aspirations in life.

He pointed to the unlit candle in the center. "This center candle symbolizes the union of your lives, the strength of your family, and your commitment to each other.

"The lighting of the center candle represents not only the union of Tom and Sarah in marriage, but also the unity formed in this new family in which your individual lives will now shine even brighter together than they did separately.

"Each candle represents your life before this day—the parents you had before, the individual lives with all its mistakes and all its glories. Each of your lives is individual, unique, and special. Please take the candle with your name on it and together light the center candle to commemorate the union of your individual lives. By joining as a family you bring your special gifts to make the family brighter and stronger."

The four of them carefully lifted their tapers and pointed it at the wick of the large center candle. When the fire blossomed, they put the individual tapers back in its spot.

"Do you see how your individual candle is still lit?" The pastor asked.

The boys nodded. Connor seemed to pay special attention, not taking his eyes off any of the candles.

"By sharing your flame you have gained power and strength together, yet you have not given up any of your unique and blessed selves.

"From this day forward you are a family drawn together by love and held together by devotion."

The pastor held his hands out to each side. "Let us pray."

Tom, Sarah, Grady, and Connor joined hands as they surrounded the candles.

"May the brightness of God's light shine throughout your lives as individuals and as a family. May it give you courage and reassurance in darkness, warmth and safety in the cold, and strength and joy in your bodies, minds, and spirit. May your union be forever blessed.

"Lord, we pray that you guide Sarah and Tom as parents to raise and teach Grady and Connor with love and respect. We ask that you protect this new family and keep them always in your care. Amen."

All four of them repeated the amen, as did many people sitting outside.

"May I present Mr. and Mrs. Pawlak and the children they love with all their heart, Connor and Grady Davidson."

"And you may kiss the bride," Grady yelled out.

The pastor chuckled. "Yes, you may kiss the bride."

Tom placed both hands at Sarah's cheeks and held her head for a few moments. He rubbed a thumb across the tears that lingered on her cheeks.

"I love you, Sarah Pawlak. I give you my heart, my breath, my life for the rest of my days."

Then he bent toward her, dropping one hand to her waist to pull her closer. At first he lightly feathered his kisses from one side of her lips to the other, savoring the sweet sensation of that soft give as she responded tentatively. The pressure of Sarah's hand on his head pulled his lips firmly against hers and his senses filled with the citrus notes of her shampoo as she kissed him with abandon—seeking, probing, promising. For a moment he lost himself in that sweet space between thunder and lightning, knowing his world would soon explode into a thousand sensations and he would not want to stop.

He dipped her slightly backward to finish the kiss before it forced him to sweep her into his arms and carry her directly to the bedroom. As if to prove he was not the one calling the shots, Sarah opened a little more and stole his breath, holding it for one moment before giving it back again.

Tom pulled her back to standing and Sarah held tight to his side as she looked up at him with a mischievous smile letting him know she knew exactly what she'd started.

Grady yelled. "We're married! We're finally married!"

Everyone laughed, and the boys jumped off the deck and rushed to get in line for the food. Sweetwater Canyon plugged in and started playing *Can't Help Falling in Love With You.*

Tom swept Sarah up into his arms and carried her down the stairs as she laughed at his antics. He set her on her feet directly in front of the band and pulled her in as close as he could get, leaving no space between them. As they swayed to the music, Sarah's pure voice softly sang the lyrics into his ear.

ACKNOWLEDGMENTS

No book makes its way to publication without the assistance of many people. I am fortunate to be surrounded by caring professionals—my editor, Jessa Slade and my cover designer, Christy Keerins. These two women are a joy to work with. They pay attention to my story, my brand, and my vision for the series and help me to render that as best I can.

I am also very blessed to have an amazing assistant, Adrienne Feehan. She allows me more time to write by taking on many of the organizational tasks that are necessary but very time consuming. She is the consummate professional and I don't now how I lived without her previously.

Beyond the professionals, I am fortunate to have a husband who supports me throughout the process. We live in a small space and that requires extra vigilance when I'm in my writing cave and needing complete silence. He keeps the cats busy and exercised, so I'm not tempted to play with them. He dons headphones to watch TV. He prepares dinner for whatever time of night I'm willing to eat (sometimes that is very late). Most of all he simply loves and supports me for who I am. He is there to hold me when I feel overwhelmed by all my responsibilities. And he celebrates with me for the finishing of each book and the beginning of the next one.

For the first time since I started writing novels, I had a group of fans who wanted to be part of an Advanced Reader team. These are the amazing fans who were willing to read this book, before final edits, and provide feedback on the story. I am humbled by their willingness to give their time and energy to this process.

First, a special thank you to the following members of my Advanced Reader team who went above and beyond their brief of reading the story and giving me an honest review. This special group of members also took extra time to answer story questions and they provided eagle-eyed catches on the occasional typo and missing punctuation.

A very special thank you to:

Linda Rutland
   Carol Boyle
   Sharon Smith
   Deborah Carr
   Jeanne Dembenski
   L'Norah Clarke
   Casey Murphy
   Norma Wiegert
   Wenda Bransford
   Lizeth Salazar

In addition to the work of the above women, I want to thank the remainder of my ARC Team for reading in advance and providing me an honest review of the story. Thank you Amy Fudge, Anna Anderson, Beth Korgood, Cathie Brashear, Chestine Harris, Debbie Eyre, Debbie Blevins, Denise Van Plew, Gladys Nason, Judith Cohen, Juliana Ignacio, June Nair, KC Crocker, Krysta Sjogren, Lenda Burns, Norine Fry, Patricia Meyers, Pauline Frost, Sandi Bedell, Sharon

Rainey, Teresa Whitehead, Tricia Wright, Vicki McGuire, and Zaza
Dehayni.

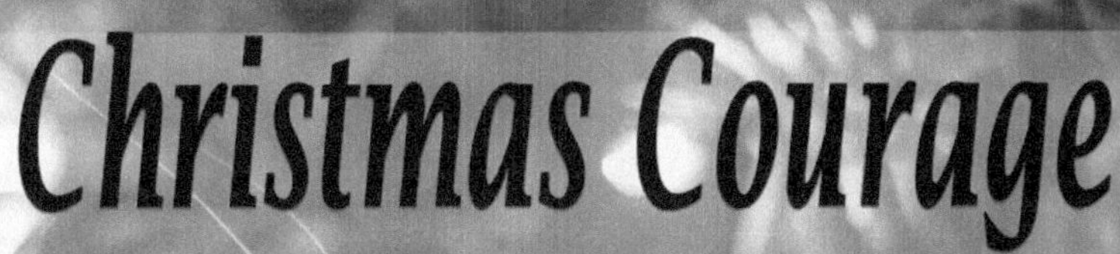

Christmas Courage

A Sweetwater Canyon Novelette

MAGGIE LYNCH

❀ Created with Vellum

Kat snuggled into the recliner and cradled her hot cocoa in her hands. The twinkling lights on the Christmas tree mesmerized her. The ornaments were a combination of shiny balls to reflect the lights, old-fashioned wooden toys, and homemade ornaments her mom had crocheted. It was the perfect tree in every way.

Was it only two weeks ago she and her mom had trekked through the snow at Frog Lake to choose and cut this Noble Fir? It still amazed her that the Forest Service let you cut your own tree, up to twelve feet tall, for only five dollars. It was the best deal ever and always an adventure of choosing the location, play arguing over which one was best, and often ending in a snowball fight before they hauled the tree back to the car and tied it to the roof.

Fortunately, the snow wasn't too deep this year and they found the perfect tree within only half an hour. The only thing she regretted was not bringing the chainsaw, as they'd done every year she could remember. Kat had watched a Hallmark Christmas movie the night before where the happy couple had cut a tree together with a bowsaw. They'd both fallen in the snow, made snow angels, and then kissed in that way only couples on Hallmark movies do—the half chaste and half OMG kiss. The movie made it all look sooooo easy. She told her mom she wanted to cut the tree the old-fashioned way this time. After Kat promised her that she would be the one kneeling in the snow and working the saw, her mom gave in.

It hadn't turned out quite as romantic as she'd thought after twenty minutes of working the bowsaw back and forth through the six-inch trunk. Evidently, the saw wasn't all that sharp. It was left over from her Dad's tools that hung in the garage untouched for the past fifteen years. It kind of made her feel good to use the saw though.

In the end, the tree really was perfect. A twelve-foot Noble Fir, with its thick, silvery-green needles and sturdy branches protruding straight from the trunk was perfect for ornaments. Though no handsome man stood by for the congratulatory kiss, Kat figured it was good practice just in case she had the chance to do this with someone else in the future. She just hadn't found her Hallmark prince yet.

Kat put her cocoa aside and inhaled the rich, woodsy aroma of the tree. She couldn't help striding to the tree to finger a lacy, starched snowflake hanging at eye level at the center of the tree. It had a picture of Kat as a baby. Born on December 3rd, her Mom had crocheted the ornament between feedings and naps in celebration of Kat's first Christmas. Then she'd made a new one every year for Kat's birthday. She looked at another crocheted ornament, a circle. This one had her baby picture for her 2nd Christmas. She worked her way around the tree until she reached the newest one—the one she had received for her seventeenth birthday. It was different than all the others. It had three balls hanging together inside a three-dimensional crocheted sphere. The first ball had a picture of Kat as a baby. The second ball had a picture of Kat today. The third ball had a question mark. Her Mom said that was for Kat to place the picture in ten years from now, when she'd made her own future.

Kat's eyes misted as she looked at it again. Ten years seemed like forever—especially since she wasn't sure about anything in her future. There was no boyfriend. She wanted to go to college, but she wasn't sure where or how she would afford it. She also wasn't sure she could leave her Mom alone in the house. Though she'd tried for years to get her Mom to date, she'd steadfastly refused.

A loud pounding at the front door drew Kat back to the present. The three cats scrambled toward the door to investigate, jumping over each other as if the first cat there would win. Who would be visiting at nine in the morning on a Saturday? Sweetwater Canyon didn't have a rehearsal scheduled today.

"Kat, would you get that please," her mom yelled from the bathroom. "Whatever the kids are selling, tell them we don't need any more wreaths or ornaments or candy or…whatever it is."

"Okay," Kat yelled back.

She looked through the sidelight to see a man she didn't recognize. He looked kind of old, maybe fiftyish. Maybe it was the salt and pepper hair. His boyish face didn't match his age. He waved tentatively and smiled. Kat unlocked the deadbolt but kept the chain on as she opened the door a couple of inches.

"Whatever your selling, we aren't buying," she said, echoing her Mom's instructions.

The man laughed and it lit up his eyes. "I'm not selling anything, Kathleen. I'm here to see you. You've grown up since I last saw you."

Kat's eyes widened. "How do you know my name? No one calls me that except my mom."

He smiled again, this time though his eyes looked sad in opposition to the smile. "It's been a long time. I don't expect you to remember me. I'm your father."

Kat froze. She couldn't speak. She stared at the man—a person she'd always wanted to meet and know more about. A person her mother had made clear she had no idea where he was or if he was even alive. A person who had never bothered to contact her in any way.

"I…uh…think I should have handled that better," he said. "Can I come in?"

Kat slammed the door and threw the deadbolt. "Mom!" Kat yelled as the panic welled inside her. "I need you, like right now!"

Her Mom ambled toward her from the kitchen. "Don't be so dramatic, Kat. Who is it?" She unlocked the door and threw it open.

"Hello, Theresa," the man said.

"No! No, no, no, no." Her Mom slammed the door closed again, threw the deadbolt in place and stood with her back at the door as if it would assure it couldn't be opened. Then she slumped to the floor visibly shaking.

Kat sat quickly beside her and reached around to hug her tight.

"I'm not leaving," the man yelled through the closed door. "I have a right to get to know my daughter."

"Mom..is it…really…my Dad?"

"No no no no no. Not now. Not without warning. This is not fair. Not fair."

"It's okay, Mom. We don't have to let him in. If he's going to hurt us I'll call the police and they will come take him away. Just tell me what you want me to do."

After several minutes, her Mom stopped shaking. "Oh, Kat. I don't know what to do. I really don't know."

"You've never really talked about him, except to say he left when I was two years old. Is he a bad man? Did he beat you? Was he a womanizer? You've never said anything about him. You don't have to protect me, I can take it. You know I can. Just tell me the truth."

Her mom let out a big sigh. "No, he wasn't a bad man to me the three short years we were married. I loved him and we made you together, the best thing that ever happened to me. But when he left without even a note as to where he was going or why, I was lost. I had a two year old baby, a part-time job, and I didn't know what to do. I kept hoping and waiting for him to return. I thought maybe he was just overwhelmed with being a father. Maybe he just needed a break and would come back. After months became years, I gave up."

"He never wrote? Ever?"

"No." Her Mom placed her hands gently on Kat's shoulders. "I'm sorry, honey. I just didn't know what to tell you. I didn't want you growing up thinking you were unloved. It was easier not to tell you anything than to say how I felt. I never wanted you to think he didn't love you."

"Obviously, he doesn't love me," Kat said. "I don't care about that, right now. All I care about is you." She held her mother's hand. "What about his family? Did you know them, did they have anything to say about where he was?"

"His mother died when Doug was twelve years old, and his stepfather was not a good man. He was someone Doug never talked about or had any contact with since he ran away at sixteen. He was an only child."

They sat holding hands in silence and Kat wondered what she should do. She didn't know this man at all, and if her mom didn't want her to get to know him, she would honor that. After all, it was her mother who had stuck by her all these years. She'd been both mother and father. When Michele got married, David became a kind of surrogate father for her. When Rachel got married, Noel became a second surrogate father. And now that Sarah was married too, even though they lived far away in Oklahoma, it was like she had three amazing men in her life. She really didn't need a father any more.

Her mother had handled the single-parent life without complaint as far as Kat could remember. From the time Kat was ten until she entered high school, her mom had worked two jobs. One as a waitress at ZigZag Pizza and another cleaning houses for people on the mountain who rented out their vacation homes. She'd juggled shifts so that she could pick up Kat from school every day. They'd go home and she'd want to know about everything Kat had learned. She also volunteered in the classroom: helping with reading circles; bringing cookies or cupcakes for special events; and occasionally even going on field trips.

Kat didn't really know about dating when she was younger, but as a teenager she'd asked her Mom several times about why she wasn't dating. Mom always said she didn't want to waste a single minute with a man when she had all the wonderful things to do with Kat. One time Kat asked Rachel about it, because she knew Rachel would tell the real truth. Rachel said that good looking single women were often not trusted because wives were afraid they'd go after their husbands. That made it hard for single women to find women friends in their neighborhood. If it weren't for the band, Kat knew her mom probably wouldn't have any close women friends.

The door shook behind them with pounding again. "Hey, it's getting cold out here. Come on, Theresa, let me in so we can talk. I came a long way to make up for everything."

"You don't get to waltz into our lives fifteen years later without warning, Doug," her mom shouted through the door. "If your cold go away. You seem good at that."

"Ooooo, good one, Mom." Kat raised her hand in a high five invitation and her Mom returned it with a wan smile.

"This isn't about me," her mom said. "What do you want to do, honey?"

"I…uh…I'm not sure. I kind of always wondered what my dad was like. But, if you don't want me to talk to him, then I won't. I mean you've been the one who stuck with me."

Her mom squeezed her hand tight. "I love you more than anything, Kat."

Kat squeezed back. "I know."

Her mom stood and pulled Kat up with her. "Okay, let's introduce you to your father."

"Really?" Kat worried her bottom lip, unsure if this was the right thing to do.

"Yes, really." Her mom hugged her tight. "This may be the only time you will ever have with him. I don't want you to always wonder what would have happened. I'm sure you have lots of questions and you can only get them answered by him." She let go and looked Kat in the eye. "Honey, guard your heart a bit. Okay? I know you always think the best of everyone, and that's a great quality. Just remember we don't live in a Hallmark movie. I don't know that he's going to stay. I honestly don't know anything about him any more."

Kat nodded. You bet she wasn't going to just open up and tell him everything. He had to prove himself to her. She also had to be sure he could never hurt her mom again.

Kat opened the door. Her father was sitting on the porch facing toward the drive. His shoulders were slumped forward. He straightened and turned slowly as he stood. "Does the prisoner get a hearing?"

"Whatever jail your in, is of your own making," her mom said. "You can come in, but I get to say when you leave."

The man nodded.

"I can't call you dad," Kat said as she held the door open wide. "So, I'm going to call you Doug. As far as I'm concerned, I've had no father."

Doug nodded again. "That's fair. I hope I can change that."

"Don't count on it." Kat closed the door behind him with a resounding thump.

"You can have a seat on the sofa." Kat pointed toward the living room. "Anything to drink?"

"Coffee?" He asked.

"I'll get it," her mom said. "You two can get acquainted while I make a new pot."

Kat took in a big breath and sat on the far end of the sofa opposite her dad...um Doug. She'd have to remember to call him Doug at all times. This was not her father in any real sense of the term, she reminded herself. In fact, her relationship to this man was even less than her relationship with the grocery store clerk she saw every week in the checkout line.

She tucked her feet under her on the sofa as she sat cross-legged. Though she'd longed for a father throughout her childhood, she always figured it would be a step-father—someone her mom fell in love with. Someone who was happy that Kat came as part of the package too. She'd never imagined her biological father would show up again. In fact, she'd pretty much told anyone who asked that he was dead as far as she knew.

"I imagine you have a lot of questions," Doug said. "So go ahead and ask them.

"Where have you been all my life?" Kat blurted out. She choked back any apology for her boldness.

Doug swallowed. "I see you have your mother's penchant for not beating around the bush."

"Trained by the best." Kat looked toward her mother and caught her stifling a laugh. "So, tell all…start with when you left us high and dry."

"Hmmm. That may take a while."

"I'm here, aren't I?" Kat tried to smile in an accepting-way, but only managed what her mom called her Mona Lisa smile.

"I'm so glad I found you and that we have a chance to get to know each other."

Her mom handed him his coffee and took a seat in a chair opposite the sofa, her arms tightly crossed at her chest and her back stiff.

"We'll see how much getting to know you I can stomach," Kat said. "Stop stalling. Start talking."

First I owe you both an apology." Doug looked directly at her mom. "I didn't know how to be a dad. I barely knew how to be a husband. As each month passed, I believed I would screw it all up. I believed I would become my step-dad and one day just be angry and bitter and who knows what I would have done."

Kat looked at her mom for confirmation or a question, but she sat still her lips locked tightly together.

Kat turned back to him, ready to defend her mom to the ends of the earth. "Did you even bother to talk it over with mom?"

"No, I didn't," Doug said in a whisper, his head bowed. "I only knew I had to leave and I didn't want to be questioned. I knew if I tried to talk about it, your mom would talk me out of it."

"Of course she would," Kat said. "That was the mature thing to do. She never thought about running away—even when times were really tough and we weren't sure where we were going to live or how we were going to eat. She always did what she needed to do for us, because she loved me."

Doug looked around the room. "It seems you did well for yourself. A beautiful cabin in the woods, on a river, warm and cozy and—"

"No thanks to you," Kat interrupted him. "The only reason we have this home is from an inheritance when grandma died from cancer. Before then, we were moving from one dingy apartment to another, barely making ends meet."

"I'm sorry," Doug said. "I didn't know. If I had, I could have…"

"Could have what?" Kat asked, her voice getting more shrill. "Could have sent money? Of course you could have, except you didn't bother to let us know you were even alive, right? What if something had happened to mom, huh? I could have been put in foster care. I could have been dead, for all you cared."

"Now that's a little dramatic, Kathleen. Things worked out just fine. I'm sorry you had some hard times."

"Right, sure you're sorry…now. But that doesn't make it right. You need to realize that actions have consequences. Mom has taught me that. It's not just the running away, it's the never contacting us too that has consequences."

"It wasn't as bad as all that, really, was it? Teens are prone to exaggeration."

"It was that hard," her mom stated in a booming voice as she stood. "Don't you dare question Kat's veracity. If this is what you came to do, you might as well leave now." She pointed toward the door.

Doug held both hands, palms outward. "I'm sorry. You're right. You're right." He turned back to Kat. "You're right, all actions have consequences. Any excuses I have in my head pale in comparison to what you had to live without my help. Again, I'm sorry. I wish I could take it back, but I can't. It's in the past."

Her mom slowly sat back in the chair. Her eyes were half closed, like when she was questioning Kat after a lie. Her jaw locked down hard. Kat turned back to Doug, ready to try again.

"And what about me?" Kat asked, her voice low. "Did you even think about me at all over the years?"

"Of course, I thought about you, Kathleen. I've thought about you every single day for the last fifteen years."

Kat sighed as she shook her head. "Now you're lying. If that's the way this is going to go, we might as well stop right now."

"I'm. Not. Lying."

"If you were truly thinking about me, why didn't you get in touch? Why didn't you send money or even a care package or even an anonymous gift? For all this time I never heard from you once." She turned toward her mom. "Right, Mom? He never sent me anything, right?"

"That's right, honey." Her mom relaxed a bit and stared at Doug. "Not once."

"Did he send any money to help take care of me?" Kat asked her mom.

"No. I'm sorry to say he did not."

Kat crossed her arms. "So, the truth is you were not thinking of me every day for the past fifteen years. Lie number one is debunked. Want to try again?"

"Okay, not every day," Doug admitted. "The truth is I ran as far as I could. I first went to Houston, figuring I would get into the oil business. I found a job on a rig in the Gulf of Mexico as a roustabout— that's an entry level, do-whatever they-ask kind of job. Over the years I worked my way up the ladder. My last posting was in the North Sea as a toolpusher—that's a management role where I'm responsible for all operations, costs, and safety."

"And they don't have mail delivery from the oil platforms?" Kat asked.

"They do," Doug admitted.

"And you don't make much money, right? That's why you couldn't send any because you were barely making enough to eat, right?"

"The truth is I made very good money, and the company pays everything. It's kind of like living at a hotel where they prepare meals and they have places in the complex for you to get away, go to the gym, read books, watch movies in your down time."

"So, you have no good excuse," Kat said. "The truth is you didn't think about me at all."

"No, that's not true." Doug leaned forward and tried to take Kat's hand, but she crossed her arms again. "One of the things that happens on oil rigs is that you have a lot of time to think and to evaluate your life. As I worked my way up the ladder, I realized that I'd really screwed up." He looked over at her mom. "I didn't think you would ever let me back in your life, even though deep down I still loved you."

"My love for you died a long time ago. I waited for years, thinking you would come back and explain—believing I would forgive you and we'd be together again. But then I had to let it go. I had to stop waiting for a fairytale ending."

"I'm truly sorry, Theresa. I never stopped loving you. I just felt so guilty for leaving that I didn't know how to come back without something else to offer. Then one year led to the next and the next and... well, here we are."

"Yes, here we are," her mom echoed. "What do you really want, Doug? Why now? Why after all these years?"

"I want to get to know our daughter. I want to make up for the time I've missed." He turned to Kat. "Can you give me that chance? I know I don't deserve it. I'll understand if you say no, but please... please just give me a chance."

Kat looked toward her mom, but she said nothing. She again looked at Doug. Could she get to know him without hurting her mother? Even if she did, what good what it do? She could see he needed to somehow get rid of his guilt for leaving. But what did she want? What was in it for her?

She looked at the tree and noticed a small wooden ornament with the manger scene of Jesus as a baby with Joseph and Mary looking on lovingly. It was Christmas time. She could give Doug a chance...at least a little time. He could never really be the father she wanted as a child. She was practically an adult now. But, maybe he could prove he was a good man. Maybe she could make a space in her life for him while he was here.

"Okay," she said. "I'll give you a chance."

Doug let out a breath in a whoosh. "Thank you, Kathleen."

"If we are going to be talking at any length, you better start calling me Kat. The only time anyone calls me Kathleen is when Mom is mad at me."

Doug chuckled. "I'm definitely not mad at you. So Kat it is." He smiled. "Thank you, and I am going to make everything up to you. I wasn't lying when I said I made good money—really good money. I haven't spent much of it. Never remarried, didn't do a lot of traveling except when they forced me off the rigs for breaks. You asked if I thought of you. I did, but I didn't know how to show it. But I do now. I've been putting aside money for a college fund for you. It's now big enough that I can afford to pay for four years of college, including housing and food expenses anywhere you want in the world."

"Wow." Kat's mouth dropped open as she thought of all the possibilities that opened up. "That's…that's really generous of you."

"It's just a start," Doug said.

Her mom stood stiffly. "Kat, I want to talk to Doug for a minute, please. In private."

"Um…okay." She raised an eyebrow. "I'll go upstairs to my room."

"Bye, Doug." She waved her fingers at him as she ascended the stairs. "I hope you aren't in too much trouble. I hope to see you again tomorrow."

She walked up the stairs wondering what Doug had said that made her mom mad this time. She was obviously mad and about to tear into him. She entered her room and closed the door loudly, then opened it again just a crack so she could hear. No way was she going to miss out on the fight.

"Oh, no you don't," her mother's voice wasn't loud but definitely mad. "You do *not* get to show up after no contact for fifteen years and throw money around to buy Kat's love. We've managed without your money for all this time and we will continue to manage just fine. Go back to your oil rig and just forget about us. That's the life you chose. You gave up your right to a relationship with your daughter a long time ago."

"I'm not trying to buy her love," Doug insisted. "Kathleen said you had a rough go of everything I just want to help."

"She doesn't need that kind of help! You don't even know her. Do you even know what she wants to do with her life? Do you even know if she wants to go to college at all?"

Kat couldn't hear a response, she opened the door a little wider.

"That's right, you know nothing about her. You don't know she's an amazing musician—she sings and plays three instruments. You don't know what her childhood was like. You don't know how much she's been hurt by a past boyfriend. You don't know that she will probably graduate summa cum laude from Sandy High School and will get a scholarship to several colleges. You don't know that she loves movies, that she believes the best of everyone, that she loves deeply and without reservation. You don't…"

Kat could hear her mother's sob and then a long silence. Kat silently scooted out the door, along the wall to the edge of the loft so she could hear better.

"I'm not trying to take her away from you," Doug said. "She'll always love you."

"I only have six to eight more months," her mom said. "Then she'll be off to college somewhere. There is so much yet to say, to do, to prepare her for being an adult. I want every minute with her I can have."

"I'm not going to take up that much time," he said.

"Aren't you?" her mom asked. "The more you get to know her, the more you will want to be with her. Then you will want to take her away for a week for a father-daughter bonding vacation. Or you'll want to show her the world, take her to Europe or Australia or anywhere in the world. You can afford it and I can't. Then time will dwindle away and I won't see her anymore."

Kat wanted to shout over the railing that she didn't have time to take all those trips either, to reassure her mom she wouldn't let him take her anywhere. But that would reveal she was snooping.

"First, I only have until December 28th to spend with you. Then I have to be back in the North Sea. I was hoping I could come back again in the Spring and maybe plan to attend graduation. While I'm gone we can correspond or do Facetime on the Internet and talk about what that will entail. And, of course, any trip we take away from home, you can come too."

"I can't afford it," her mom said. "Obviously."

"I'll pay. It only makes sense that you would have to come too. You are Kathleen's mother."

"I don't know," her mom answered. "I don't know if I can do that."

"Don't make up your mind right now. Just think about it. Right now, I have no trips planned for father-daughter bonding. I haven't thought that far ahead. I didn't know if you'd even answer the door once you saw me. All I know is I want to spend time getting to know Kathleen… and you too, if you'll let me. It's only a week until Christmas. I would love to be part of her life this week, if you'll allow me."

"I suspect she would like that too," her mom said. "Wouldn't you, Kat?" Her mom yelled toward the loft.

Busted.

"Sorry, Mom. I just couldn't help myself."

"Come on down and be part of the conversation."

Kat hurried down the stairs, speaking as she made her way. "Yes, I would like to have Doug here and get to know him, but only if it's okay with you."

She hugged her mom tight. "I love you. I love you. I love you. I'll never stop loving you."

Her mom laughed. "You heard that part too, then?"

Kat nodded as she felt her cheeks warm. "Mom, no one can ever make up for the past. I have every memory in my brain of all the things we did together. Just look at the tree." She pointed at it and looked at Doug. "Every crocheted ornament is about me. Go look. Mom made all seventeen of them."

Doug walked to the tree and took his time looking at each one.

"That's just the memories I can see today," Kat said to her mom. "But there are much more carried in here." She touched her palm to her chest. "No one can take those away. No one can replicate them because it was only you and me who made them. And there will be lots more. You'll be there when I find the love of my life. You'll be there when I have babies and I get to see you be a grandma. And I don't know how much else is going to happen, but you will always be there."

Her mom pulled her tight to her side. "How did you get to be so smart?"

"Your genes, Mom. And the fact you never once let me skip doing homework."

"Do you have luggage with you, Doug?" Her mom asked.

"Yes. I was hoping you could recommend a hotel," he said.

"If you are going to maximize the short time you have, you better stay here."

"Really?" Kat asked, barely able to keep herself from jumping up and down and clapping.

"Yes, really." Her mom hugged her again. "I'm thinking the basement bedroom. What do you think?"

Doug scooted toward the door. "I'll be right back."

Kat peered out the sidelight. "He has four suitcases. That's a lot for two weeks. More than me when we go on tour."

"I suspect there are presents," her mom said. "He's kind of like Santa Claus for you this year."

"Are you sure you are okay with this?" Kat asked again.

"I'm fine. Besides, when the rest of Sweetwater Canyon comes over for Christmas, they'll give him the once over. If he survives that, I'll have a little more faith in his promises to you."

Kat laughed.

"Honey," her voice turned serious. "Don't get your hopes up about this going anywhere in the world for college business, okay? I don't know if he's really thought it through or really has the money."

"No worries, mom. I don't even know where I want to go. That's for next year to think about. Right now I only want to think about Christmas."

CHAPTER 3

Theresa was up early on December 24th. Today the Sweetwater Canyon women and their families would be coming to celebrate. It was tradition to spend Christmas Eve at Theresa's house, then Christmas day with their own families. She'd warned them about Doug, and she still did want to see how he interacted with all of them. They were her found family, and the only family Kat had ever known. It was critical that Doug understood that.

She heard Kat in the bathroom upstairs, and quickly busied herself making the pancake batter and getting the hot water for coffee started. It was also tradition to start Christmas Eve day with a pancake breakfast.

"Yummm." Kat said as she sidled up to her mom. "Which mold are we using this year?"

"Which one would you like?"

"The Christmas tree, so I can decorate it with blueberries and whipped cream." She snatched a handful of blueberries from the bowl in the fridge and popped them in her mouth.

"If you eat them all now there will be none left for your pancake."

Kat giggled and opened the fridge again. She withdrew a bowl of strawberries. "I'll work on these then."

Theresa laughed. "Help me set the table and knock on the basement door to wake up your dad."

Kat popped another strawberry in her mouth before wandering down the basement stairs.

The past week with Doug had been interesting. In some ways he was the same man she had fallen in love with all those years ago—charming, fun, easy to be around. In other ways, he was very different. Definitely more confident and he knew what he wanted in life now. He seemed to genuinely love his job, even though he admitted to not having any social life.

Theresa wondered if she might have any feelings left for him at all. When he'd left so long ago, in spite of many offers, she didn't date because she truly believed Doug would come back. Three years later, when she'd finally given up on him, she was too busy working two jobs and taking care of Kat to even have energy to date. Then it just became a habit not to think about romance as one year moved into the next. Now, at 42, she pretty much figured the best time for romance had passed her by. Not that she was too old. It's just that she didn't think she could compete with all the young women out there. She had friends who'd been married for 30+ years and then suddenly divorced when their husband found a new, young girlfriend. She'd decided it was better to just live her life with Kat and not worry about relationships. It was a lot easier not to put her heart out there again.

"Mmmm. Is that fresh ground coffee I smell?" Doug asked from the top of the basement stairs.

"Yes," Kat said, rushing to the French Press. "I know how to make it too, with this. On Christmas Eve and Christmas Day, Mom has special coffee with vanilla nut and infused with a bit of chocolate."

"Do you drink coffee?" her dad asked.

"No. Mom says I don't need the caffeine. And she's right. I'm pretty hyper anyway. But I luuuvvve the smell." Kat inhaled deeply before pouring the hot water over the grounds, giving it a little stir, and setting the timer for it to steep.

Kat moved to the stove where the batter was already prepared and the mold was in the pan. "We're making pancakes that look like Christmas Trees. Do you want me to make you one?"

Doug looked over her shoulder. "Looks good to me. Who knew I would have daughter who could cook. You definitely don't get that from me."

"From Mom," Kat said. "She started teaching me to cook when I was four or five, right Mom?"

"Yup. First cookie batch you helped make was your fourth birthday."

"And I spilled a bunch of M&Ms on the floor." Kat carefully poured the batter into the mold. "I think I've improved a bit since then."

"Did you ever learn to cook, Doug?" Theresa asked.

"Afraid not. One of the nice things about working offshore platforms is it comes with a chef to prepare all the meals. When I'm not on the platform, I'm staying in hotels."

"Not even frozen TV dinners?" Kat asked.

Doug laughed. "Yeah, I can do those. I can read directions and push numbers on the microwave. But I only do that when I'm staying way out in the country."

"Like here," Kat said.

"If I were here alone, it would definitely be frozen waffles for breakfast, ready-made salad for lunch, and TV dinners at the end of the day. Thank goodness I can rely on you two for real meals."

Kat removed the mold and flipped the pancake over with ease.

"Wow, just like a pro," Doug said. "Mine would be all over my shirt or the floor if I'd tried that."

Theresa smiled as she watched Kat place the pancake on Doug's plate and carefully decorate it with blueberries on each branch and then followup with an artistic rendering of whipped cream to look like snow all over the tree.

"It looks too pretty eat," Doug said as Kat offered him the plate.

"Okay, I'll just have to eat two then." Kat snatched it back and put it on the back of the stove.

"Nope." Doug stole it from the stove. "In that case I'll have to sacrifice your artwork to my stomach first."

Kat laughed and playfully chased him to his seat.

"You're next, Mom." Theresa's pancake was quickly served and Kat was readying her own.

"Thanks, sweetie." Theresa pressed the coffee and served it, carrying two cups to the table. "I assume you still take it black?"

Doug nodded.

Kat soon joined them both with her pancake and chamomile tea. "I'm really glad you took a chance on finding me," she said. "This past week has been awesome."

"For me too." Doug squeezed Kat's hand. "I promise I won't wait so long for next time. "Is it okay for me to come to your graduation?"

"Absolutely! And I really hope I get to be the Valedictorian. I already have an idea for what I want to say."

"Really?" Theresa asked. "I didn't know you were already thinking about that."

"Yup, but it's a secret."

Theresa rolled her eyes. "Everything you do is a secret these days."

"I love surprises, and this week has been the best surprise ever. So, it will be my chance to surprise both of you."

"What if you aren't the valedictorian?" Theresa asked. "I know you could be, but sometimes it's a tie as to who is top of the class."

"Then I'll be salutatorian or some other 'torian. Or, I'll just have to do my speech for everyone at the house afterward. Believe me, you will get stuck hearing it no mater what."

CHAPTER 4

Theresa looked at her watch again. Four o'clock. Everyone would be arriving for Christmas Eve dinner in the next half hour. Her only responsibility was the ham. Everyone else would bring the vegetable, candied yams, and pies. The oven timer went off and she bent to the oven. She hoped the ham was absolutely perfect.

"Can I help you with that?" Doug asked behind her.

She pulled the ham out and transferred it to the counter to rest. "Wow. It's gorgeous. Do I really have to wait to have a slice?"

Theresa laughed. "You never were very patient." She checked to see that the cloves were all still there. It really was one of the prettiest hams she'd ever baked. The glaze was perfect. The dark corn syrup had given the ham a deep rich brown color. The cloves had opened the ham's aroma and the honey glaze offered a sweetness that was hard to resist. She could barely stop herself from picking off a piece to taste it.

"If you're willing to do the slicing, I'll look the other way if you snitch a piece in advance."

"Deal." Doug took the knife and large fork from her and laid it near the cutting board. "How long?"

"About ten minutes."

As Doug worked on slicing the ham, people started streaming into the front room. Kat directed food to the table. Theresa took jackets, sweaters, and scarves and everyone started talking at once. It was exactly the big, busy family Theresa loved having to her home every year.

Doug appeared at Theresa's side. "Done with the slicing. I put it on the table with the rest of the feast. Anything else?"

"Let me introduce you," she said.

"Attention." She raised her voice but it seemed no one heard. "Attention," she said again.

Kat let out a shrill whistle. "Always works." She smiled. "Mom has something to say."

"I'd like to introduce Doug Fraser. Kat's father." She went around the circle, naming each member of the band, their husbands and children.

"Can't promise I'll remember all your names," Doug said. "Kat has been prepping me all week, so I at least have the band members down. I hope I get a chance to talk with each of you during the evening."

It devolved into everyone talking at once again, until suddenly Theresa was cornered in her bedroom by Michele, Rachel, and Sarah. Rachel closed the door.

"Give us the truth," Rachel said. "How crazy mad are you about Doug showing up."

"I was beside myself at first. But as the week has gone on, I see it as a blessing."

Michele touched her arm. "Are you sure? I know if my old boyfriend had shown up at my house I'd have shot him."

"No you wouldn't," Sarah said. "You are not the violent type and you don't know how to shoot a gun."

"Okay, figuratively. It was a metaphor for how angry I would have been." Michele squeezed Theresa's hand. "Are you really okay? I mean with him staying here and everything?"

"You don't have to pretend with us," Rachel added. "You can scream and yell and swear if you want to and we will do the tar and feather treatment, sending him off in a way where he won't ever want to come back."

Theresa smiled. Her bandmates were the best family ever. Willing to protect her at all costs. "Really, I'm fine. I didn't know how much blame I'd been holding onto all these years. Not knowing why Doug left made me think of all the things I might have done wrong. And now…well he's the same rogue, charmer I fell in love with but more mature. He's actually a better man than he was before."

"And are their sparks again?" Sarah asked. "I didn't think I could ever even look at Tom again, but now were married. Is that how things are headed now for you—after this past week?"

Theresa shook her head. "No. There is no spark at all."

"Because you can't forgive him?" Asked Sarah.

"No, I've actually forgiven him, though I haven't exactly said that yet." Theresa said. "Even though he's a nice guy, and he's finally coming through with being a great father to Kat, I just don't have that connection with him anymore. The chemistry just isn't there. I'm so different than I was before—more confident. I know more what I want…what I need in a partner and he's just not it. Right now, he feels more like a long lost brother. Someone I care about, but not in a romantic way at all."

"That brother thing is definitely not good for romance," Michele said.

"Exactly!" Theresa agreed. "Over the past week I've realized what a gift it was for Doug to return. Not just for Kat, but for me too. I won't ever think about the what-ifs with Doug anymore. I know it's not there for me, and that is really freeing. You know?"

They all nodded in unison.

"As for Kat, I couldn't be happier. Doug and Kat are good for each other. Most of all, Kat can now enter adulthood knowing her father did love her after all. I know she's been carrying some guilt too, wondering if it was her fault that he left. She's wondered if it was because she was a horrible two year old. Can you imagine?"

"She didn't need to carry that around," Rachel said. "She's been through enough in her young life. If he has in some way given her more confidence, then I'm glad Doug came back too."

"We better get back to the party or the men will think we are cooking up something they won't like in here," Theresa said.

As if by magic, the bedroom door opened and Kat poked her head in. "I'm starving, mom! Can you all continue your conversation about my dad later? We need to eat."

They all laughed. Rachel patted Kat on the head. "From the day I met you, you've been starving. Yet here you stand five years later."

DINNER WAS RAUCOUS, fun, and consisted of lots of teasing mixed in with holiday compliments. Kat and her dad shared clean up duty in the kitchen as everyone else settled into the living room. When they were done, everyone joined in the living room for Christmas carols, with the Sweetwater Canyon band providing the music. Soon, the five children were falling asleep and carried downstairs to be snugged into sleeping bags in the second bedroom in the basement. Ranging from age two to ten, it was amazing they all got along so well.

Theresa snuggled into her chair, enjoying the conversations around her. Kat soon joined her.

She bent to Theresa's ear. "This was the best Christmas yet, Mom."

"It's been pretty amazing," Theresa agreed. "I don't know if I can top this next year."

"You don't have to top it. Just be here when I come home from college."

Theresa patted Kat's hand. "I'll be here anytime you come home. Even when your fifty. As long as I'm alive I'll be here."

"What if you remarry? You might have to move then."

"No. This is my home. Anyone who I love will have to agree to live here."

"Mom, don't you think that's being kind of selfish? What if you fall in love with someone in Paris? Or Wellington? Or maybe even Rekjavik?"

Theresa chuckled. "Are you watching a lot of the Travel Channel now? What makes you think I would fall in love in any of those far off places? And Rekjavik is way too cold."

"Okay, not Rekjavik. I'm just saying you don't have to stay here forever. I'll be able to find you no matter where you are."

"What's this about, Kat? Is Doug luring you to some far off place?"

"No, mom." She drew out the 'mom' as she sighed at the same time. "It's just I'm thinking about college now and I'm considering Ireland or Scotland."

Theresa sat up straight. "Really? Why those two?"

"Well, most of the music we play is roots music and even Americana has roots in Irish and Scottish tunes. So, I thought it would be amazing to live there and go to college and be able to jam with musicians there all the time."

Theresa's heart seemed to flutter as she imagined Kat living so far away. She'd always known Kat would go to college, but she thought it might be Portland State or maybe as far as Corvallis or Eugene. She'd never really thought about her leaving the country. But now with her father's money, that was a possibility. She had no idea how she'd manage living truly alone.

"I think that's a good plan," Theresa finally managed to get out without letting her fear into the words."

"Really? You would be okay with that?"

"Of course, honey." She hugged Kat's side with one arm. "I want you to do whatever you think is best for you. And now you have the means to do it."

"But I'm worried about you," Kat whispered.

"Why? There's nothing to worry about."

"I kind of hoped you would have fallen in love by now and, if not married, have someone else in your life. Then I wouldn't have to worry about you being alone."

Theresa sighed. Had she been the kind of parent who held on so tight her daughter felt she had to stay there forever? She'd never intended that. She remembered an aunt who never married because her mother was widowed and she felt the need to stay with her. It seemed like a sad life. That wasn't the life Theresa led. Was it?

"I won't be alone," she finally said. "I'll still have Earl, Doc and Emmy Lou to keep me company."

"Mom, cats are not the same as a husband or lover or whatever you call it when you get old."

Theresa chuckled. "Calling me old is not helping your cause."

"You know what I mean. I just want you to think about finding someone before next fall. Then I'll be able to go to college and not have to worry about you."

"Honey, love doesn't happen just because you wish it. I may never remarry, and I'm fine with that. You don't have to worry about me. Besides the cats, I also have Rachel and Michele and their families nearby. And when we tour, Sarah will join us too. I won't be lonely."

"Just try to fall in love, okay?"

Theresa chuckled and patted Kat's knee. "I'll do my best."

Connor burst through the door from the basement. "Help! Help! Tamara is lost somewhere in the snow and Claire went after her. You have to help."

CHAPTER 5

 $\mathcal{E}$ veryone jumped from their chairs at once. Michele and David hit the basement steps first, running down them two at a time. "What happened? She was asleep. What happened?" Michele kept asking.

When they got to the bottom of the stairs, everyone was talking at once. Tom finally cornered Connor and hugged him.

"Quiet everyone!" Tom yelled. "Okay Connor. Now take a deep breath and tell us what happened. It's okay, just tell us the truth."

Connor shook as his father's hand attempted to steady him at the shoulder. "We were all asleep and we thought we heard a cat meow outside. I turned on the light, on the patio, and looked but I couldn't see anything. So, I told everyone to go back to sleep. Tamara was sitting by the slider and she kept saying a baby kitty was crying. I kept telling her no, it was something else. But she kept sitting there. After a while my eyes got tired and I fell asleep. Then I woke up and thought I heard it again. I looked around and Tamara wasn't there. Then Claire got worried so she put on her coat and went out to look. And then she disappeared too and now I'm worried they are both frozen somewhere."

Rachel rushed up the stairs and brought down all the coats she found on the bed in Theresa's room. She quickly put her coat on and started out the slider door.

"Rachel, wait!" Noel shouted. "Wait for me."

Rachel stepped back inside. "Hurry. It's below freezing out there."

"Everyone wait," David said as he put on his coat. "We can't all go rushing out there. Someone needs to stay with the other three kids."

"I'll stay," Theresa offered. "I'll stay in case they come back and you miss them."

"Good. Thank you," David said.

Connor zipped up his coat. "I'm going with you. I can help."

"Not this time, son," Tom said. "I think we have enough people to search. You need to stay here and help Theresa. If Claire comes back with Tamara, or one of them comes back alone, Theresa will need your help getting her warm or doing first aid. You know first aid, right?"

"I learned it in boy scouts," he said proudly.

"Exactly why you need to stay," Theresa patted his shoulder. "I need you here with me."

"Okay." He shrugged out of his coat with some reluctance. "I'll stay and help Miss Theresa."

The other adults were all suited up now.

"Let's go," Rachel said. "I can't just stand here anymore."

"Theresa, get your cell phone," David said. "I have mine with me. If anyone comes back before we do, you call me. Okay?"

"Okay, I'll go upstairs and get it now. You guys head out."

Kat raced up the stairs and was back down before the others left. "Here, Mom." She threw the cell phone toward Theresa. "I'm going with them." Then she stepped out the door to join the party.

David had everyone synced to a map on their cell phones. "Michele and I will take the section to the west beyond the park and down to the river. Noel and Rachel, you take the middle section from the park boundary to the west and over to the edge of the next house and down to the river. Tom and Sarah, you take the eastern section. Doug and Kat, you take the section moving south, from the front of the house to the gate and cover the entire circle of houses inside."

"We should agree to how we call and when we listen," Tom said. "If we are all calling all the time, we may not here a response."

"Right," David agreed. "Can we do one minute of calling and 30 seconds of listening each time?"

"Got it." Everyone echoed.

"Let's go, first minute of calling then 30 seconds of silence," David said. "Do not lose site of your partner."

They all headed in the designated directions calling out the names of Tamara and Claire, then silence to listen for 30 seconds. Then calling again.

After an hour, David called the Sheriff's office and asked for help. He called each of the teams and asked them to come in as well.

"Something's not right," Kat said as they turned back to the house. "Everyone else had a larger area to search. If the kids could hear a cat's meow and followed it, they wouldn't have wandered to the river. It's too noisy. It's hard to hear anything out here really."

"What are you thinking?" Doug asked.

"I'm thinking it's closer to the house. Cat's like to be warm. They aren't likely to go wandering in deep snow unless they are really scared. Even then, once the fear passes they would want to be some-where warm."

"Where should we look? It's your house."

Kat checked the perimeter of the house, but couldn't find any hiding places. The basement was a walkout, and the foundation was cement brick and hardy plank siding. Nowhere for a cat or a kid to get in. She looked again around the backyard. What was close to the house that might be warm?

"The wood pile!" Kat ran toward it and the plastic tarps covering the six cords of wood still left to burn. She put a finger to her mouth to signal quiet. She kneeled on the ground and crawled slowly along the edges.

"It's too cold out here," she heard Claire say. "We need to hold onto each other to stay warm."

"Kitty needs to be warm too," Tamara answered. "Poor kitty."

Kat raised the tarp where she heard the voices.

"Kat!" Claire jumped up and wrapped her arms around Kat's shoulders as she sat in front of Tamara.

"Just a minute," Kat said. She pulled out her cell phone and hit the picture of her Mom. "Mom, we found her. Call everyone and tell them to come to the wood pile. Tell Connor to suit up and bring two blankets out to me."

"Hi, Tamara," Kat said as she removed her own coat and wrapped it around Tamara as best she could. "What are you doing out here?"

"The kitty was crying." She lifted up her little pajama top and a small baby kitten was tucked underneath asleep in her lap. "Now she's not crying anymore."

"That's good," Kat said. "Why don't you get up and bring the kitty inside and we can all take care of her?"

"She can't," Claire said. "She's stuck." She pointed to the stack of logs on both sides of Tamara. "That big tree branch there." She pointed to the one resting with one end on the wood stack and the other hung up by a small tree branch. "It fell when I found Tamara and knocked the piles out of wack." She pointed to spots on either side of them where the entire log pile had shifted forward from the impact of the falling branch.

"Whenever I try to move her, the logs start falling. See there?" She pointed at several that had fallen to fill the hole above their heads. How it was balancing was anyone's guess. Kat moved up slightly to make sure she was over Tamara's head in case something fell. The slightest bump in the wrong direction could bring everything crashing down. A branch that size could kill Tamara and probably Claire and Kat too.

"I see the problem," Kat whispered as she swallowed down the fear.

"So, I decided to stay here and just talk to her," Claire continued, "until someone found us and could get help."

"That was very brave of you," Kat said. "Help is on the way."

Doug bent beside Kat. "So, this is the cat rescue club?" He removed his coat and put it around Kat's shoulders.

Kat nodded. "We can't move any of the logs without protecting

Tamara." She pointed to the problem logs on both sides. "I'm afraid if one falls, they will all tumble down."

"Let's get Claire out of here first then," Doug said.

"I don't want to leave Tamara," Claire said.

"It's okay." Kat gave Claire her hand. "I'll stay right here until David comes. Nothing will happen to Tamara."

Claire rose slowly and stood. Two logs on the other side teetered dangerously. Doug came around to Claire's back to protect her if anything fell. He slowly helped her edge away.

"Okay, Claire, can you go wait over there?" He pointed to a tree about 10 feet away. "I want you to stand on the other side until your mom and dad get here. Okay?"

Then he bent to Kat. "How about if we change places? I'm bigger than you and can offer more protection."

"I don't think so," Kat said. "Tamara knows me, not you. She might get upset and that wouldn't go well. Besides, I don't know if you can fit in this tiny space."

"Then you don't mind if I just hover, do you? I don't want to lose you when I've just found you again."

Kat nodded, her eyes watering from the realization of how amazing this week had been—finding her father, getting to go to college without worrying about money. All she had to do was live through this little spot of trouble.

"I'm tired," Tamara said. "Can we go home now?"

"As soon as your mommy and daddy get here. Okay?"

"I want to go now." She started to stand, and three pieces of wood fell on Kat's back pushing her into Tamara. Then a big roar as others tumbled around them. Doug's head fell against her side and she heard something crack, then the rest of his body collapsed with the giant tree branch on top of him.

"Dad?" Kat reached toward his hand. It wasn't moving. "Dad?" She asked again. "Are you okay?"

Nothing. Silence.

Tears streamed down her face. It couldn't be. She couldn't lose him now. Now that she'd just met him.

"Tamara?" Michele's voice was above them. "Kat? Are you okay?"

"Mommy!" Tamara screamed and cried. "I want out, Mommy. I want to go home now."

"Mommy's going to help, sweetheart." Kat could hear the tears in Michele's voice. "You just stay still okay. Just a few more minutes. Is Kat with you?"

"Yes, Mommy."

"I'm here," Kat said. "My Dad. How is my Dad?" She couldn't keep her voice from shaking.

"He's alive," David's voice answered. "Don't move. The ambulance is on the way. We can't move anything until the ambulance and the rescue crew gets here. The log is too heavy and I don't know if it will rain more wood on you and Tamara."

"Please help him," Kat whispered. "Please don't let him die."

"I want out, Mommy. I want out now!" Tamara screamed again.

"Tamara." Kat stroked her head. "How is the kitty? Is the kitty okay?"

Tamara choked on her last sob and lifted her shirt to take a look. "Yes, see. Still sleeping."

Kat placed a hand on the kitten, it was warm but it's breathing seemed pretty shallow. *Dear God, don't let the cat die,* she prayed. *All this will be worth nothing.*

"David," she called out.

"Yes, Kat?"

"Call the vet. If this little kitten dies I think we will have a flood on our hands."

"Okay, Michele is calling the vet now. Who knows if she will come out here on Christmas Eve or if she's even home.

I hope so, Kat thought to herself. It seemed that kitten's life was the thread that held everything together. Tamara, Kat, and her father.

"Kat, can I go home now?" Tamara asked. This time her voice sounded much more tired.

"Not too much longer. So, what is the name of your kitty?"

"I don't know. She didn't tell me yet. She just crawled on my lap and then went under my shirt and went to sleep."

"Should we call her Lappy, then?"

"That's not a name," Tamara said. "You made that up to be silly."

"How about Shirty?"

Tamara giggled. "No. She needs a brave name. She was all by herself—no mommy or daddy—too small to get out of the deep snow. She needs a brave name."

"Okay, a brave name," Kat echoed.

Kat heard several sirens come to a stop on the road. Then too many footsteps to count hurrying toward them. A deep voice issued instructions for people to assemble all around the wood pile. Each person was assigned certain things to lift or hold or push. Kat couldn't make it all out to really know what was going on.

Everybody was being brave today, Kat thought. This little kitten probably would have frozen to death without Tamara finding her. Tamara could have been unconscious or even dead without Claire finding her. Yes, everyone was brave, and it was all because of this little kitten.

"Duck your head and hold on," David called out. "We are all lifting logs at the same time. Courage, Kat. You and Tamara duck, hold tight, and old onto your courage."

Kat pushed Tamara's head into her lap as she bent over her. Courage. That would be the cat's name.

The ground seemed to shake and the wood moved all around her. Kat wanted to cry out in fear, but she couldn't. All she could do was pray for everyone—her father, Tamara, herself, and little kitty, Courage.

Hands reached in and grabbed Kat and Tamara at the same time. Tamara screamed and little Courage fell from her lap. Kat lunged and caught the kitten in her hand. A woman's dainty hands gently took the kitten. Kat looked up. It was Dr. Houston from Barlow Trail Vet Clinic in Sandy. They'd found someone to come out on Christmas Eve. Dr. Houston had cared for all three of their cats for the past five years.

Kat turned just in time to see her dad loaded into the ambulance.

Noel stepped to her side. "That was a very brave thing you did, Kat. You saved both Claire and Tamara."

"What about my Dad," she asked. "He saved me. He has to live."

"It's hard to know right now," Noel said. "But he's a strong man. He's unconscious. He probably has some internal injuries. We won't know the extent of his injuries until they get him to the hospital and the ER doctors to some tests."

Kat hugged Noel tight. "Take care of Claire," she said. "Take her home and keep her safe."

"You should go inside and see your mother," Noel said. She's worried sick too.

"I will, in a minute." Kat rushed to the car where Dr. Houston stood. The vet wrapped the kitten in a blanket and laid her in a small carrier on the floor in her car.

"The kitten's name is Courage," Kat said before the doctor closed the door. "Please tell me she's going to be all right. She just has to be. If she lives, everyone lives."

"I don't understand," Dr. Houston said.

"I don't either, but it's all tied together." Please save her.

"I'm taking her home and I'll feed her with a dropper. I'll call you tomorrow and let you know, okay?"

"On Christmas? You're willing to call on Christmas?"

"Of course, Kat." Dr. Houston said. "I think it's time for a Christmas miracle. And it will happen if each person does their part."

CHAPTER 6

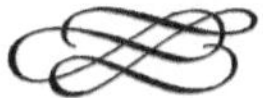

"**K**at." Theresa shook Kat's shoulders. "It's time to wake up. It's Christmas."

Kat turned over and pulled the blanket over her head. She was afraid to wake up. Afraid that Courage would be dead and it would unravel everything good from the past week.

"Come on, Kat." Theresa shook her again. "It's noon. Everyone's waiting on you."

"Who is everyone?" Kat mumbled.

"The whole family."

"What do you mean?" Was she dreaming? The whole family was Theresa and herself.

Then she popped straight up. "The *whole* family?"

Theresa nodded.

Kat raced out of her room and leaned over the loft bannister. All of Sweetwater Canyon was there. Everyone who had been there last night. But what about her dad? He was family too. She didn't see him.

"Look." Theresa pointed to Rachel and Noel.

Tamara waved at her, then lifted her shirt. Courage was sitting on her lap, but instead of sleeping she was looking up at Kat.

"Alive! Courage is alive," Kat yelled as she hurriedly tripped down the stairs and ran to Tamara. "How?"

Michele smiled. "Dr. Houston called the shelter looking for a cat that was still nursing kittens. It turns out, the shelter had given away all the kittens but no one had taken the mother cat yet. So, Dr. Houston took the mother cat and put Courage with her to see if the mother cat would let her nurse. She did. In fact, she started licking her and protecting her like a good mother."

David reached behind Tamara and brought out a small white cat with black markings. "So now we have two cats," he said. "Courage and a foster mother."

Kat couldn't stop the tears in her eyes as David put the mother cat to one side of Tamara and little Courage immediately snuggled in to nurse.

"What should we name the mother cat?" David asked.

"Houston," Kat said, her voice still a little shaky. "After Dr. Houston who saved the kitten."

David hugged her tight. "You and Tamara saved the Kitten." He paused for a moment and she heard the choke in his throat. "And you saved Tamara."

Kat didn't speak for a moment. Is it possible one more miracle would happen today? "Then, Dad is okay too, right?" Kat asked. It had to be. If Courage lived, her Dad had to be okay.

Theresa came behind her. "Yes, he woke in the hospital this morning. The doctors said he was very lucky. He has two broken legs and a couple of broken ribs, but that's it. We can go see him this afternoon. And, I'm afraid he'll be staying here longer than he planned. At least eight weeks while he heals."

Kat smiled between her tears and kneeled in front of the nursing cat. "Courage brought us all a Christmas miracle."

MAGGIE LYNCH

A
Sweetwater Canyon
Novelette

The Hogmanay Stranger

Windtree Press

https://windtreepress.com

The Hogmanay Stranger / Maggie Lync. -- 1st ed. ISBN 978-19423685-7-1

❀ Created with Vellum

CHAPTER 1

Rachel paced in the conference room beneath Michele and David's condo in the Pearl District. Sunshine played peek-a-boo with the clouds over the Willamette River as yesterday's storm blew eastward. When David first took over booking all of Sweetwater Canyon's gigs each year, he used his office at home. But soon, they were doing so well that he hired a part-time assistant and took over an office downstairs.

With only two months until the holidays, she had a special funding request and David Blackstone was the man with the purse strings. Because of his management and marketing capabilities, Sweetwater Canyon was finally making a living with their music. No more break-downs on the road. No more wondering if they would return home even more broke than when they left. No one was a millionaire, or even a hundred thousandnaire—except David with his consulting business—but no one was starving either. Each woman had sufficient income to survive on her own if needed.

Rachel's da had sent her an invitation to come home to Scotland for Hogmanay. She hadn't been home in eight years and she was dying to go. Letters and Google Hangouts had kept them in touch, but nothing like seeing each other in person. Her da had invited the entire band and their families to his home and B&B in Dunoon, Evie's Inn, named after Rachel's mother. Hogmanay was a traditional time to welcome friends and strangers to your home, and to enter into the new year together with a clean break from the past—looking forward, not back.

Rachel wanted to share Hogmanay with both her families—her da in her family home and with the family she'd come to know in America since she'd joined Sweetwater Canyon five years ago. If she didn't extend the invitation and work out the financing now, they would all make other plans. The logistics could be difficult, but that wasn't her prime worry. It was the cost to fly all five women and their families to Scotland during one of the busiest travel times of the year that had her prepared to beg for assistance.

David sauntered into the conference room and smiled. "So, what was so important you had to call me away from Michele and little Tamara? I can't believe it was only a few months ago she was barely walking on her own. Now I can hardly keep up with all the places she finds to climb and get into trouble."

He turned and reached into the small refrigerator for a pitcher of water. "Can I offer you any?" he said, holding a glass next to the raised pitcher.

"Sure." Rachel ran nervous fingers through her hair.

He looked at her with narrowed eyes. "Is there a problem? Where's Noel?"

"Noel's home with Claire. No problem...exactly." Rachel shifted from one foot to the other. "I have more of a question. I need an advance or a loan or something."

"Have a seat." David placed the glass in front of her on the conference table and sat in a chair facing her.

She flopped into the chair and then sat erect, her fingers drumming on the table. She hated asking for favors but this meant the world to her. Somewhere deep inside she knew it was important to spend Hogmanay with her da. She didn't know why this year was more important than any other, but it was. This was the first time he'd actually extended the invitation. He hadn't made it to her wedding, hadn't even met Noel yet. Though she and her da loved each other, since her maw's death they'd been a bit closed…not as forthcoming in their conversations. Rachel saw this opportunity as the first real chance they had to define a new life without her maw.

She had left so soon after her mother's death, and then been consumed with her new husband, moving to America, his infidelities and the divorce a few years later, that she'd never had the time—taken the time—to reconnect with her da. It had been eight years since she'd been able to hug him. Now with Noel and Claire and a real family of her own it seemed even more important.

She wanted, no needed, this time for the two of them to discover how they could both move forward and still be a family together and part of the extended family she now shared. She very much wanted Claire to know her Scottish roots and especially her grandfather. She also wanted her da to be a regular part of their family—more than a person seen a computer screen once a month.

David took a long, slow draught from his own glass of water. "Are you and Noel having financial problems?" He asked, his voice soft.

"Oh, no. No, no, no. It's nothing like that." Rachel clasped her hands together to stop her fingers from tapping." Da wants us to spend Hogmanay with him."

"That's great." David tilted his head and quirked an eyebrow. "Isn't it?"

"Oh yes. Absolutely. Claire is thrilled and can't stop talking about it, and Noel has never been to Scotland and I'm excited to share it with both of them, but…"

"But?"

Rachel took a deep breath. She'd talked about this with Noel, but she still hated asking for an advance. It's just that she wanted to make it a present for everyone, and they couldn't do that easily on his teacher's salary and her usual take for the band gigs.

"Rachel?"

"The deal is I'd like to take everyone with me. Our family home is also a B&B and Da will put everyone up and have meals and all that, but I wanted to pay for the airfare so no one would feel they couldn't come because they couldn't afford it."

David nodded slowly. "I see."

Rachel rushed on. "I don't want to sound like I always hit you up because your…well…you know…rich."

David nodded. "We are very comfortable."

"I know you and Michele can afford it for sure, but Theresa is trying to pay for Kat's college and Sarah and Tom are still deciding what to do about the ranch and have lots of bills for rebuilding and it didn't seem fair that I would pay for some and not others, so I figured I'd just pay for everybody but I can't exactly afford it and so I'm asking for an advance or a loan or whatever you think is right."

David chuckled. "You're sounding like Kat with that sentence going on and on."

Rachel let out the breath she was holding. "I just don't like asking." She purposely paused and took another breath. "But all of you are my family too. You've been my only family until I met Noel and I just can't imagine spending New Year's without all of you. And it's the first time I'll be home since maw passed, and I'm not sure how I'm going to take it or how da will be about it. They were engaged on Hogmanay you know." She swallowed against the lump in her throat and the memories of her mother's illness and having to leave so soon after her death.

"It's not a problem." David covered her hand with his. "Let me pay for everyone as my Christmas present to the band."

Rachel stood. "No. That's not what I meant. This is why I didn't want to ask. I knew you would do the rush in and save us thing just like you did when Annabelle broke down."

"I'm not saving anyone and, if I remember correctly, it was that motorhome breakdown that provided me with the best opportunity ever—marketing for the band and getting Michele back in my life. I've been thinking what to do about gifts. It's been such a wonderful year and this is the perfect way to celebrate it—all of us, together, in Scotland. I can probably even book a couple of gigs to help pay for it all."

Rachel shook her head. "Admit it, this is much more than you would normally spend. We are talking thousands of dollars to fly everyone there. No, I want an advance or a loan. My idea. My treat."

"What if I can get a couple gigs?"

"I don't want us worrying about playing during the holidays. I just want us to enjoy each other. We can sing and play if we want, but nothing formal, nothing that we absolutely have to do." She paused and stood still, looking out the window. This part of Oregon even reminded her of Scotland. She had to share it with everyone. She turned back to David. "Please, lets do this my way for once."

David shook his head in resignation. "Why are all the Sweetwater Canyon women so stubborn?"

"We have to be because we seem to fall in love with stubborn men." Rachel smiled. "Thanks for the offer though. Now, how are we going to arrange this?"

David reached for his computer bag and pulled out his laptop. "Let's see what we can do." He typed something on the keyboard and then nodded. "Here's the deal. Michele and I will pay our own way."

"No. I want to be fair. I pay for everyone."

"If you want my help, Michele and I pay our own way. I'm not charging you for a loan to pay for something I can do on my own. Also, with Tamara, we will be wanting to go first class or business class to have more space and some sleeping room."

Rachel let out an audible sigh. "Okay. I can accept that."

David nodded. "I will make all the arrangements for everyone so we can leave at the same time and arrive at the same time. If we get the tickets together we can get a group rate. Also, I can use my miles to get upgrades for everyone to at least business class."

Rachel thought about arguing on the miles but she knew she would lose that one too. Besides he probably had enough miles to last him for years. She had to admit that traveling in business class would be a lot more comfortable than coach.

"Thank you," she finally said. "So, you'll let me know the damages and the terms of the loan?"

"I will. I'm estimating the charges will be somewhere between three and five thousand dollars. That's about two months pay for you on our current schedule. Shall we say three years at no interest?"

"No. That's not fair," Rachel said. "The bank would charge me a lot more than that."

"I'm not a bank," David said. "I'm family. You just said so yourself."

"But even family deserves interest on a loan. Business is business. How much would you be making on that money if you didn't give it to me?"

"That's not the point."

"How much?" She asked again.

"Two percent."

"Liar. You would have it in some great stock that is making gagillions."

He chuckled. "You must think very highly of my investments. There is no stock that makes gagillions."

"Okay, an exaggeration. But I know two percent is not realistic."

"This particular money is in a money market account. That keeps it liquid. Money market interest right now is less than one percent. So, by charging you two percent I'm gouging you. Do you feel better now?"

Rachel narrowed her eyes and studied him. She had no idea what money market rates were right now. "Deal." She finally held out her hand. "Shake on it."

David shook her hand. "You'll also sign a promissory note. You wanted this to be business."

"Thanks, David." She looked straight at him. "Really. Thanks. This means a lot to me."

CHAPTER 2

*R*achel stared out the window of the limousine hired to bring them all from Glasgow airport. She didn't know how he managed it, but as usual he had everything arranged to make the trip as easy as possible. She watched for her home as the hired car lumbered up the steep winding drive to the top of the hill. Positioned high amid a woodland garden, the home—now Inn—enjoyed sensational views over the Firth of Clyde.

Claire dozed curled on Noel's lap. Both Kat and Theresa had drifted between reading a book and napping during the hour ride. Michele held a sleeping Tamara while snuggled into David's arm. The two-year-old had been so good on the long flight that Rachel had almost forgotten they had such a young child with them. Sarah and Tom snuggled together in the last seat at the back. Still newlyweds, it seemed they couldn't stand to not be touching for even a second.

Noel squeezed Rachel's hand. "You okay?" He whispered.

She nodded. "A little anxious."

"It will be great." He drew her closer into his side. "With all your friends here, there is nothing that can happen that we can't handle together."

She gasped as the view of the house appeared in the window.

The main house still fronted the firth. It's three-story Victorian structure loomed tall on the steep hill. The bright white stucco, trimmed in black, presented a happy welcome. It was much better than the slate blue and grey she recalled when she'd left Dunnon with her ex-husband and worried that her father had to face his grief alone.

The limousine came to a stop and Rachel scooted toward the door to be the first out. Her father appeared at the top of the drive and her breath caught. He looked good. Healthy. Smiling. Not much different except more grey in his hair. She ran to him, tears streaming down her face.

He wrapped her in his big strong arms. "I missed you Rachel. I'm so happy you could come and bring your friends."

She buried her head in his chest, inhaling deeply the smell of pine boughs and firewood that she always remembered for this time of year. Why had she taken so long to return home?

After a minute, her father released her. "Let's meet your husband and daughter. Shall we?"

She turned and Noel and Claire were right in front of her, waiting quietly. Noel held out his hand. "Good to meet you sir."

Her father shook Noel's hand heartily. "Gavin. Please call me Gavin. Sir makes me feel old."

"Gavin then." Noel smiled and knelt on the ground to be at the same height as a sleepy Claire. "Claire, this is your granda. "

Claire looked up shyly. "You talk funny, like mommy."

Gavin laughed. "Aye. I do, lass. And you talk like an American."

"I am American," Claire said.

'That you are. Let's get everyone settled shall we?"

Rachel introduced all of her friends and their family.

"Leave the luggage for now," Gavin spoke to the group. "We'll get it sorted shortly after all the rooms are assigned. We have the entire Inn to ourselves for Hogmanay."

Rachel helped direct each family to their room. Claire went with Noel to unpack in a room with a queen bed and a small side room with a twin for Claire. Michele and David were in a room next door with a child's bed for Tamara. Sarah and Tom were one level up, and across the hall were Theresa and Kat, each with a double bed.

All the rooms were taken except the one small one in the back corner, facing the hill. It was originally designed as a housekeeper's quarters. To her knowledge, Rachel's father had rarely rented it except in emergencies when a traveler was stuck late at night with nowhere to go. Rachel thought it could serve as a quiet place to get away from everyone else if needed.

When all were settled in rooms they reconvened in the living room.

Claire ran to the Christmas tree festooned with packages. "Mommy, does Santa come after Christmas to Scotland? Nobody opened their presents here."

"For many years celebrating Christmas was banned here," Gavin said. "That means we were not allowed to celebrate it publicly."

Claire wrinkled her nose. "You mean Santa wasn't allowed to come?"

"Santa still came, but in secret," Rachel answered. "When I was a little girl, Santa came on New Year's Eve. We call that Hogmanay."

Claire laughed. "That's funny. Hug muh nay? What does that mean?"

"It means many things," Gavin said. "In olden times, the solstice was celebrated by the Celts and the Vikings and many other cultures. They called it *oge maiden*, meaning new morning. It is when the shortest day of the year is past and from that point forward the days get longer. The solstice usually happens just before Christmas, around December 21st. However, because of disagreements between the Church of Scotland and the Catholic Church long ago, the public celebration of Christmas was banned. So, instead we celebrated on New Year's Eve—when we say goodbye to the old year and welcome the new year. *Oge maiden* over hundreds of years became Hogmanay."

"It is also called *hoog min dag* or the great love day. " Rachel added and winked at Noel. "You will see," Rachel looked around the circle of friends and family. "We'll be participating in many of the traditions over the next few days."

Gavin looked at the clock above the fireplace. "It is time for dinner and then I bet you are all tired from travel and want to get bed early. Best to get your sleep now. Tomorrow is the last day of the year and all the celebrations will keep us awake through the night and into New Years."

~

AFTER ALL WERE SATED with food and off to their rooms to sleep, Rachel curled up in one corner of the settee in front of the fire, her hand draped along the armrest. Her father occupied his usual large leather chair to her right, a glass of Talisker in his hand. The day had gone well. Claire and her granda had hit it off, and Noel was quietly comfortable with him. Her da seemed relaxed, happy.

He took a swig of his whisky. "Your family seems to fit you well," he said.

Rachel smiled. "Yes. Noel and Claire are more than I could have ever wished for. I didn't know how much I needed them until they came into my life."

They both looked to the fire in companionable silence.

"I 'm sorry I…" they both said at once.

"You go," they both said at once again.

Her father reached over and placed a hand on her arm. "Please, you first."

Rachel inhaled a deep breath and let it out slowly, concentrating on not letting go the tears filling her eyes. "I'm sorry I didn't write more, left so early, couldn't talk about mum. I feel like I let you down."

Her da immediately moved to the settee and drew her into his chest. "It is I who let you down, Rachel. I knew Kavan was not the man for you, but I was so lost in my grief I had no energy to fight about it. Then you were gone to America and it was as if I lost my daughter too."

No longer able to hold back, Rachel weeped into her father's shirt. She cried for all they had missed together. "You could never lose me, da. Never."

When she'd stopped crying, he gently pushed her away from him and ran a thumb beneath her eyes to dry the last vestiges of tears. "Tomorrow is Hogmanay. We will purify the house together and put our grief in the past. I've been waiting to do this and now that you and your family are here, it is right to move forward."

Rachel nodded. "Are you done grievin', Da?"

"One is never done," he said. "But it does not hurt as much as it once did. And it is no longer every day that I long for her. I will always have the memories of your mother as a vibrant, loving woman. Eight years is a long time to grieve. It is time to move forward." He paused and let out a sigh. "How 'bout you lass, are you done grievin'?"

"The same as you…I think. Though with leaving home and all that has happened, I fear I have perhaps moved on faster. I fear…perhaps… I forgot things too soon."

He patted her hand. "No, not too soon. You are young. It is right that life is alive for you. There is no need to dwell on the past."

"Do you think…" Rachel paused. She couldn't ask that question. It wasn't her place.

"I know what you ask, lass. I have thought of it often myself. I believe Evelyn would want me to love again. But I admit I haven't been looking. There are a couple women in the village who have set their caps for me, but I canna think of them that way. It will happen when it's right. How would you feel about it, Rachel? Would it hurt you if I met someone?"

Rachel looked into the fire. Her father deserved to find love again. She'd had her second chance already and he deserved the same. "I want you to be happy," she finally said. "It will be strange, I suspect. But I know you would only choose the finest woman and how could I not love her too?"

"Aye," he said and clasped her hand with a smile. "I will let ye know when I find her."

CHAPTER 3

*K*at tiptoed down the stairs in the early morning. Her sleep cycle was completely bonkers now. The eight-hour difference was driving her batty. They were eating dinner last night at lunchtime and going to bed at dinnertime. Now it was five in the morning, but back home it was prime time for date night. Ugh. There was no way she could sleep.

She quickly wrote a note to her mom, so she wouldn't think she'd been kidnapped in the middle of the night or something. She placed it on the fireplace mantle where it would be easy to see. She shrugged on her raincoat and galoshes near the front door, tucked a paperback novel under the coat, and carefully let herself out. A strong wind added more chill to the already moist air. She'd been hoping for snow, like they had on Mt. Hood back home. Evidently the weather in Dunoon was very similar to the weather in Portland. Rainy. Who would've known?

Pulling the hood tighter around her face, Kat thumbed the flashlight app on her phone to help see the gravel path in the dark. If there was a moon tonight, the clouds obscured it. She could see a few lights on the firth below, but not many with the misty fog hanging over the harbor. She turned toward the back and slowly made her way down to the greenhouse where Rachel's father kept all the plant starters. It would at least be dry and warmer in there, and she loved sitting alone, surrounded by plants and reading a good romance novel.

Hmmm. The light was already on inside. Someone must have forgotten it when they took the tour of the property yesterday afternoon.

The door creaked like the opening of a horror movie when she opened it. She couldn't stop her heart from automatically beating faster. "Silly," Kat said aloud. "We are in a tiny village in the early morning. There aren't going to be bad guys in here." She laughed a little anxiously at her wandering imagination.

"Maybe there are," a male voice responded and she jumped back and screamed.

A hand snaked over her mouth from behind. "Don't do that," he said. "I'm just teasing, I'm not a bad guy."

Kat stomped on his instep, just as she'd been taught in self-defense class.

He yelped.

She grabbed a trowel from the table next to her and brandished the pointy end at his throat. "Who are you? What are you doing here? This is Cullen property and I'm sure you don't belong here."

The man didn't look much older than Kat—maybe eighteen instead of seventeen. Hard to know. His longer, shoulder-length hair curled naturally around his face. His clothes looked a bit ragged. Jeans with holes in the legs, a flannel shirt that looked like it came from the Goodwill bin. Did they have Goodwill in Scotland?

"I would appreciate you not stabbing me with that," the young man said.

Kat did not change the position of the trowel. "I said who are you?"

"Nobody. Just looking for a warm place to spend the night."

"Nobody is not your name. Who are you?"

He lifted his hand slowly, palm facing the pointy end of the trowel. "I can talk better if I don't think you are going to cut my throat with that thing and infect me with whatever dirt or other chemicals it has on it."

Kat waved it side to side. "Talk."

His hand grabbed her wrist and twisted until she dropped the trowel. He kicked it under the potting bench.

"Why you…." Kat couldn't think what to say. "I'm leaving now. I'm going up to the house and reporting you."

The young man grabbed her wrist again. "Please don't do that. I'll just leave."

He looked so tired and downtrodden that Kat couldn't help but think he was either running away from home or homeless.

"I suggest you let go of me or I will scream my head off and then you'll never leave."

He let go and headed for the door. "I'm outta here."

She ran ahead and stood in front of it. "Wait! Maybe I'm being a little harsh." What was she doing? He might be a murderer and she was asking him to stay? This never turned out well in the movies. "It's cold and rainy out there. Where would you go?"

"Just a minute ago you were threatening to cut my throat and now you're acting all Mother Theresa?"

Kat waved a hand in front of his face. "Look, I was just taken aback…you know I didn't want any Jason, Friday the Thirteenth stuff happening. It was just a reaction. But I'm not like the innkeeper who puts out baby Jesus when there's no room, either. You know?"

The guy laughed. "You are somethin' else. Americans are always so…weird."

Kat pulled herself up straight. "Look I'm trying to help you here and you're gonna trash talk my country?"

He shook his head and held out his right hand. "Let's start over. I'm Ian. You are?"

Kat worried her lower lip. Finally she shook his hand. "I'm Kat. We're visiting Rachel's Dad. Mr. Cullen. We're staying at his place. Well the B&B place I guess. We're all in a band together and Rachel recently got married and so did Sarah, and before that so did Michele, and well we are all like family, but were not, but we are are. Do you understand?"

"I'm not sure I do, you talked so fast I might need a translator."

Kat laughed. "You're funny. I'm the one who needs a translator with that accent."

"Your in Scotland, lassie. This is how we talk. You're the one who has an accent."

The door rattled behind her and they both jumped. Ian's eyes grew wide.

Kat slowly turned to see Gavin's large frame fill the door.

"Your maw's worried about you," he said, not looking at her but at Ian. "Who's this then? How did you get to meetin' a lad already? You've barely been out of my site except after we all went to bed."

"It's not what ye think, sir," Ian said.

"Then what is it?"

Kat stepped in front of Ian and shook her head to warn him not to get in trouble.

Ian pushed her behind him again. "I was crashin' here to keep warm," Ian said. "I'm sorry. I'll go now. Happy Hogmanay to you."

Gavin stopped him with a strong hand to his shoulder. "Have you nowhere to go lad?"

"I do." Ian responded. "I do."

"And where would that be?"

"Um...east of Dunoon. I'm going' to meet my sister but got a late start and got a bit tired and saw the greenhouse and thought to get out of the wind and rain."

"Did ye now?"

"Yes, that's it," Kat offered, now standing side by side with Ian. "And I got up early 'cause I couldn't sleep and came down here to read and here he was."

"And what's your family's name, lad? I know most everyone in these parts."

Ian swallowed, his eyes darting to one side and then another as if looking for escape.

"I see," Gavin said. "Your on your own then. How long? You best tell me right."

Ian let out a big breath. "My da kicked me out when his lady friend came home last week. He said there wasn't enough room for her and me and I were old enough to be on my own."

"And your da is?"

"It doesn't matter now, does it? He doesn't want me back." Ian kicked at the gravel.

"You're welcome to stay with us if I have his permission, lad. But I'm not harborin' a runaway. So, tell me who he is and I'll go round and talk to him."

Ian said nothing his eyes cast down.

Kat pushed at him. "Tell him, Ian. If you're telling the truth, Gavin will take care of it. I know it."

Ian looked away. "It's McKay. It won't do you any good to talk to him."

"Your father is Calum, then?" Gavin's voice lowered.

"Yes, the same. The one that is in the papers every week." He looked up and locked his jaw. "I'm not like him, Mr. Cullen. And I'm not goin' back no matter what you say and no matter what my da says. So you might as well just let me go now and be done with me."

"Don't be so anxious to get out in the cold, lad. I understand it all now. How old are you? Sixteen? Seventeen?"

Kat stared straight at him. She wanted to know too.

"Seventeen and ready to work."

Gavin clapped him on the shoulder. "We'll see about work after the holidays. You come with us for now. It happens I have a small room left in the inn. You bring us good luck this day. A stranger at our door. So you come on up and get some breakfast and I'll get you settled. Then you can help us get ready for Hogmanay."

Ian didn't move. Kat saw him swallow several times. She didn't know who his father was, but Gavin evidently knew him and he must be bad enough that he wasn't even going to go talk to him.

"I've got to get breakfast started," Gavin said. "Kat, you see that Ian here gets back to the house. " He looked at Ian. "I'll find you a clean t-shirt and you get washed up for breakfast. We'll talk later about what you can do to work for your room and board." Then he turned and walked out the greenhouse door.

Kat couldn't stop smiling. "See. I told you Gavin would take care of everything. I knew Rachel's dad would be cool, but he's even better than I thought. You know his wife died eight years ago, right? I mean he's been running this place pretty much on his own. I'll bet he's really looking forward to the help and all."

Ian didn't respond, but he followed her without hesitation as she led the way back up the hill to the main house. Who would've known that an early morning visit to the greenhouse would end with a handsome boy staying at the Inn? She smiled, barely stopping herself from skipping her way up the hill. This might be an even more amazing new year's then she thought.

CHAPTER 4

Theresa paced the floor in the room she shared with Kat. After hearing Kat's story over breakfast she was still seething. How could Gavin take in a perfect stranger, especially with Kat here? Kat had always been a bit too accepting of people but Theresa had never considered she would have to be protecting her against some hoodlum in Scotland.

A solid knock on the door stopped her pacing. "Come in."

The door opened and Gavin stood in the frame. "From your terse instructions, I gather you are upset."

"Close the door," Theresa mumbled. "I don't want everyone here to be listening to us."

Gavin closed the door behind him but didn't move further into the room.

"Look at it from my perspective," Theresa started and began to pace again. "If Kat were your daughter and you were visiting America and a strange boy with a criminal family history accosted her, would you be happy if I then invited that same boy to stay in my home where he could convince her to do who knows what?"

"Because the father is rotten it doesn't mean the boy is too," Gavin said. "He's a lost lad with nowhere to go and little skills to survive. Would you have me put him out in the cold?"

Theresa sat on the edge of the bed. "No, but isn't that what social services are for? You do have social workers here don't you? Don't they have special arrangements to come help those children?"

"May I?" Gavin pointed to the other bed in the room.

Theresa blew out a big breath and nodded.

"He's seventeen," Gavin said as he lowered himself to the other bed and faced her.

"Exactly, and that's a big problem. Kat's been hurt before and I don't want it to happen again. This young man is obviously a man of the world already. Kat is innocent, trusting. She see's life like one big romantic movie."

"I think you are selling her short," Gavin said. "She was ready to protect him from being sent to the police. I think she understands on some level that he comes from a bad family."

"She would. She sees herself as the savior of animals and anyone who is orphaned. That's how she sees this boy, as an orphan who needs saving—not the predator he could be."

"Predator? That's being a bit harsh."

"Is it?"

"Yes, you know nothing about him."

"I know men," Theresa said. "They all want one thing from girls."

"Really?"

She stood and looked down at him. "Yes. And it is my job to protect my daughter from them."

"I see."

"No, you don't see. I have been a single parent since Kat was two years old. I've been the father and the mother, and sometimes the big sister when needed."

"I'm sorry," Gavin said. "It sounds like it's been a rough time."

Theresa looked away and, after a few moments, sat down on the edge of the bed again. "I'm sorry. I must sound like an ogre."

"No. You sound like a mother who loves her daughter very much. Evelyn was the same with Rachel."

"I know I can't protect her from everything," Theresa continued. "I already failed her once by not being understanding of a … a particular situation. What can I do to make this Ian go away?"

"I could try to find you a place elsewhere, if you prefer," Gavin said. "There are probably no Inns with rooms but I could talk to a neighbor if you like."

"No. She would blame me for being too paranoid and it would certainly drive her back here. She would sneak out just to learn why I didn't like the boy."

"Then we are at a stalemate," he said. "It is Hogmanay. A day when the entire country celebrates. Even if social services would take him—which they wouldn't because he's seventeen—they aren't open and no offices will be open until the day after New Year's. I've known this family for a long time and I've never once seen a police report where Ian has gotten into trouble."

"That doesn't mean—"

"I promise," he interrupted her. "I promise to share the burden of watching out for Kat. I promise I won't let anything untoward go on between them."

Theresa sighed and shook her head. "I guess I don't have much choice."

"Come on, Theresa. If you give the lad a chance, you may even find out you like him." Gavin stood and opened the door. "We're going to be cleaning most of the afternoon, so now is the time to get some rest. Once the festivities start you'll be going until the wee hours of the morn."

~

EVERYONE JOINED Gavin in the living room. Ian had cleaned up as best he could. The clean shirt that Mr. Cullen had supplied hung loosely on his thin frame. Truth be told he'd never really celebrated Hogmanay. His Da had always left him at home to tend the animals while he went out and caroused. Then he'd come home sometime the next day, delivered by a friend or a woman he'd met in town, and Ian would help carry him to the bedroom. It was then he swore he'd never drink whisky because of what it did to a man.

The fire flamed high and the lights of the Christmas tree glowed brightly. While they had all napped, Ian and Gavin and two young girls had worked at cleaning the Inn from top to bottom—changing all the sheets, airing out the rooms, adding new towels, and readying the sideboard with the traditional Hogmanay meal. Ian couldn't help but count his blessings that he was here instead of home.

"Ian, will you pass out the gifts and then we will all open them together," Gavin said. "There is one for each of you."

"Da, it wasn't necessary," Rachel said.

"Of course it was. You are my guests and you must be prepared for all the celebrations to come."

Ian crawled beneath the tree and located all the packages, calling out the names and greeting each person with "Happy Hogmanay. "

"Da?" Rachel shouted when Gavin had disappeared.

He hurried down the hall from the back room with a package he handed to Ian. "It is not brand new, but it is well earned."

Ian's eyes widened. He couldn't remember ever receiving a Hogmanay gift. "Thank you, Sir," he said. "It is beyond the call."

Rachel also held out a package to Gavin. "Da, for you. I made it myself—well, with help from Theresa who actually knows how to knit."

Gavin hugged Rachel tight and Ian swallowed hard. What a family this was, filled with love—as it should be.

"Well, what are you waiting for?" Gavin asked. "Let's see what Santa brought us, shall we?"

Claire was the first to tear open the wrapping paper but was not able to cut the ribbon that secured the square box. Rachel reached over with scissors. As Claire opened the box, others began to exclaim their own surprise. Each person had been given a warm wool sweater. The women and girls received a tartan cape with the Cullen colors and the men received a tartan cap.

"The colors are beautiful," Theresa exclaimed holding the poncho in front of her, dark and light blues with small strips of green, yellow and black.

"Blue is for the Cullen family tradition as Police Officers," Gavin said. "The light blue is for the family's Scottish heritage."

"The gold is for the family's military service," Rachel added. "And the green is for their Irish heritage."

"Your family is both Irish and Scottish?" Sarah asked.

"Yes, the Gaels, what you call the Irish," Gavin said, "conquered most of Scotland around the fifth century. The language and mixing of the cultures are particularly evident today on the western coast and the highlands in smaller villages like Dunoon and in the Hebrides. It's near impossible to find a Scottish family without Irish in their blood too.

"And the black?" asked Michele.

Rachel looked at her father and answered in a soft voice. "Black is for mourning those who were lost."

"What about yours?" Claire asked, pointing at the still unopened box in Gavin's hands.

"Oh, I almost forgot." He bent low in front of Claire. "Would you help your granda open it?"

"Yes!" She tore into the wrapping with the same abandon she had used on her own present. Then she opened the box and pulled out two mittens in a navy blue color with grey cuffs. "Mommy and Theresa made them," Claire declared.

Gavin immediately put them on. "They are perfect." He wiggled his fingers and Claire laughed. "Now that everyone has warm things it is time to join the processing of fire."

Outside, behind the Inn and part way down the hill a large stone circle enclosed a six- foot basket-weave woodpile. Three-foot wax tapers were neatly stacked nearby.

"Everyone get a candle," Gavin instructed. "And the honor of the first lighted torch goes to the newlyweds."

Gavin lit the large candles that Tom and Sarah had selected. They smiled and kissed in the light of the candles, and then each helped to light others.

"Now we carry our fire and join the door to door procession of torches," Rachel instructed. "This is one of my favorite parts of the evening. We all gather together in the village and go house to house."

"Not the entire village," Gavin corrected. "We've grown a bit and have divided up into neighborhoods. But certainly we will process with our nearest neighbors."

~

Soon they joined several other families carrying torches as well. Kat compared it to a caroling party in that they went house to house and sometimes sang. But it was also quite different in that everyone had these big candles and with each house, more joined the procession. Kat walked with Ian, while her mother and Gavin walked just ahead.

"This is amazing," Kat said. "You are so lucky to get to do this every year."

Ian smiled but kept his head down.

"Is something wrong?" Kat asked. "Aren't you having fun?"

He turned around and stared down the long line of the procession. He smiled and turned back. "I've never done this before."

Kat's eyes widened. "Never?"

"Me da always went out to celebrate but that meant I was to mind the house. And…well…the procession doesn't stop at my house. People kind of avoid us."

Kat didn't know what to say. One part of her wanted to thrash Ian's dad. Another part of her wanted to hug him tight and kiss him like crazy. Instead she kept moving forward in silence.

"Sorry," Ian said. "I didn't mean to bring ya down."

"No. You didn't do that. I'm just sorry your family is kind of screwed up."

Ian let out a guffaw. "Screwed up is putting it mildly"

Kat took his hand in hers as they walked side-by-side. "As far as I'm concerned, you are part of the Sweetwater Canyon family now."

Ian swallowed hard and looked away.

Kat squeezed his hand. "I hope that's okay with you."

"It's…" Ian withdrew his hand and took a handkerchief from a pocket to wipe his face. "Good."

Though Kat was surprised at his tears, she looked away to give him some privacy. She knew he wouldn't want her to say anything. Guys were like that. Not so good with emotional stuff.

"It's not all that great, really," she said, picking up the pace as they climbed a hill to the next house. "I mean we are a bit crazy, what with the band and all, but we put up with each other most of the time."

Ian bumped her shoulder with his. "So, I have to put up with you then?"

Kat laughed. "Oh yes, more than put up with me. You have to do everything I say, and right now I say last person to the next house doesn't get any treats."

They both took off, running to the front of the line with their long candles bouncing above the others.

Each house provided a part of the Hogmanay feast and a good Ceilidh—a social gathering. At one house they offered shortbread to the walkers. The entertainment consisted of storytellers both young and old. At the next, the main meal of venison pie and a side dish of rumbledethumps—a type of potato casserole with turnips and kale and topped with cheese—fed each of those traveling with the fire procession. Then they moved to another home where music played and everyone danced and dessert was served. As they passed each house, the members of that family joined them in the procession as well.

All of the neighbors ended at the Cullen's inn with Kat and Ian being the first ones there, holding open the gate to the backyard. The long line of families rippled down the steep stone steps like water cascading over river rocks. Each person grounded their fire just outside a circle of stones surrounding a giant pile of wood. When all the other tapers were out, Gavin touched his to the kindling and paper at the bottom. It took off immediately, crackling and singing as the flames climbed to the top of the pile.

"Happy Hogmanay!" Gavin declared as he walked from one person to the next offering a dram of whisky and sharing old stories of Hogmanay past.

CHAPTER 5

*R*achel saw Kat taking a drink of whisky and then coughing. She ran to her side. "Your mother is going to kill me for this."

"Then we won't tell her," Kat responded still barely able to talk. "Besides its legal for me here."

Ian looked sheepish. "Sorry, I figured one dram wouldn't hurt. And she is seventeen."

"She may be seventeen, but I doubt she's ever had alcohol and whisky is not the way to start. And, in America the age is twenty-one so you can imagine how her mother would feel about this."

"Twenty one? I can't imagine they all wait 'til then."

Rachel sighed. She wasn't going to get into American teen ways with Ian.

"It tastes awful," Kat said, swallowing multiple times. "I don't know why anyone would like this."

"I'm glad *you* don't like it," Rachel said. "So, don't try anymore. Come on, we need to get set up. We will be expected to start playing soon." She half dragged Kat in her wake to the other side of the bonfire.

"Good neighbors," Gavin began. "I am blessed to have my daughter, Rachel, here again after eight years. She comes back with her family and her friends." He pointed to the women arrayed to one side of the bonfire. "This is the Sweetwater Canyon band all the way from America—Portland, Oregon."

The band played the traditional tunes Rachel had taught them before the trip, and they also did a few of their own original tunes. Claire joined in on fiddle as she could, and Rachel asked her father to join them with his fiddle as well. She couldn't help but tear up remembering the times she and her father would play together for her mother while she was ill.

Eventually, Rachel invited all musicians to get out their instruments and join them. She knew that Kat, Theresa, and Sarah would struggle to pick up some of the tunes they'd never heard before, but that was the nature of many Ceilidhs—musicians played as best they could, sometimes sitting out and at other times taking the lead. She'd forgotten how wonderful and warm it was to play with so many people who cherished the old tunes.

During a pause, Gavin asked, "Rachel, do you remember any of the dances?"

"Oh, I don't know."

"Please, mommy, please. I know you do. You've taught me a couple."

"Only if you dance with me," Rachel answered and took Claire onto the lawn.

Gavin started a jig with his fiddle and the other musicians joined in. Claire and Rachel stepped together. When the musicians changed to a reel, Ian sidled up to Kat and took her hand to teach her. Other dancers joined in. Soon, it was one big happy party with musicians trading off, dancers coming in and out, and people milling about having a grand time. The whisky was plentiful, but no one seemed to be over the top as they counted the minutes until midnight.

The women of Sweetwater Canyon gathered near one end of the yard for a moment of quiet with just the five of them.

"Thank you," Rachel said. "Thank you for being my family for all these years and for giving up your own New Year's celebrations to come here with me."

"To us!" Michele raised her class.

"Wait, let me refill." Rachel poured a little more whisky in her glass and offered it around the group.

"Not me," Sarah demurred.

"Come on, Sarah," Rachel teased. "One dram is not gonna hurt you. It may even loosen you up a bit."

"I don't need any loosening," Sarah retorted. "Besides it's not good for the—" She cut off her response with a hand to her mouth and all her band mates quickly closed in.

"Your pregnant?" Michele asked.

Sarah blushed and nodded. "Two months. But we weren't going to say anything until after the first trimester."

Screams of happiness welled from the group.

Gavin poured another dram for each of the men. "Sounds like we are in need of a toast," he said. He called the attention of all those gathered. "A toast to the new bairn. May he—"

"Or she," the women said together.

"Or she," he repeated, "be the light in your eyes, the lilt in your step…"

"And the longin' for the day she leaves home," Rachel finished with a laugh. "And may she not give you as many headaches as me."

The evening continued with singing and storytelling. As the church tower rang out twelve times, all the neighbors gathered round the bonfire. Crossing their arms they held each other's hands in a full circle as they sang *Auld Lang Syne*.

Ian made sure he was at Kat's side. For the first time in his life, he actually believed he was an accepted part of this community. For the first time in his life, he felt like he had a family.

He stared at Kat as she sang all the verses. Her voice pure, her eyes glistened in the light of the bonfire, and Ian marveled at how his decision to sleep in that greenhouse had changed his life. At least for tonight, he wouldn't think about the future. He would only think about now. And about Kat.

The song ended and Ian turned to Kat, softly brushing a kiss across her cheek. "Happy New Year," he said. "Thanks for trusting me. This is the best Hogmanay I've ever had."

"This is the only one I've ever had," Kat said, her wide eyes and broad smile alight with the reflection of the bonfire. "I want to come back every year!" Then she grabbed Ian and planted a strong kiss on his mouth. "Now that's a proper kiss."

Theresa scurried over. "Time to turn in," she said to Kat.

"I'd like to stay out for awhile. Please?" Kat drew out the please.

"I don't know. It's very late. It's…"

"Mom, it's not like I don't stay up late for New Year's at home. And it's not like I get to be in Scotland every day or anything."

Theresa looked from Kat to Ian and then back to Kat again. After a long pause she sighed long and loud. "All right, but don't go wandering off. Stay here by the bonfire or in the house. And no whisky! Understand?"

"Yes, Mam." Kat executed a perfect military salute then hugged her mom. "Thanks."

"I'll be out here until the fire is out," Gavin said, appearing behind Ian with a hand resting on his shoulder. "Nothing to worry about."

Theresa laughed. "You really don't remember much about teenagers do you, Gavin? They have a way of getting into trouble without even moving a step."

Kat rolled her eyes. "Mom."

"I'm going. I'm going." She hugged Kat again and then walked toward the Inn without looking back.

Gavin watched Theresa as she slowly took the steps back up the hill. Her face was strong. Her high-boned cheeks and animated fine lines in her face told of a life that was hard but had also had its share of laughter. He couldn't help but wonder in that second what his wife would have looked like at this age. She would be softer, he decided, because she'd known love. Theresa knew the love of a daughter and of friends, but not the good love of a man.

For the first time since his wife's death, Gavin felt a stirring of interest. He shook his head. An old man's folly. It would be impossible to try a long distance relationship with an American, her teenage daughter and an ocean and thousands of miles between them. He turned back and looked into the dying embers of the bonfire. It was a good thought for a few moments though. It felt good to even consider it.

CHAPTER 6

Smoke filled the room and Kat choked on the smell. She was between her bed and the wall. How did she get here? Last she remembered was saying good night to Ian and then climbing the stairs to the room she shared with her mother.

"Out! Everyone out!" Ian shouted as he ran up and down stairs and halls. "Out now!"

Her mother called out, "Kat, where are you?"

She heard hands patting the bed. Kat tried to answer but her voice didn't work. Too much smoke.

Bells rang and siren's blared.

A door opened.

"Theresa, You have to come now," Gavin said.

"I can't find her. I can't find her!" Her mother's panicked voice screamed.

"She must already be out of the house. Come. I don't know how long the structure will hold."

The door closed with a slam.

Kat fell back to sleep.

She woke again but the nightmare was worse. She could feel the heat now. Flames licked the outside of the bedroom window. She crawled on the floor to the door, but she couldn't get it open. The handle was stuck. She heard shouting as if it was far off. Maybe it was just a bad dream. Realistic, but just a dream. She decided to go back to sleep and hope that next time she woke it would be breakfast time.

Theresa shook Ian hard. "Where is she? Where is she?""

"I don't know," he said. When we turned in she said she was going to bed. Wasn't she in the room with you?"

"No! I felt the bed, she wasn't there!" She ran off to check with others.

❧

IAN STARED hard at the Inn. It had been here all of his life. It was more than one hundred years old. The left side, where the fireplace had been was completely engulfed. If Kat was in there, he hoped she was on the right side, where her room had been.

He looked down the hill where the local fire truck was still lumbering slowly around the turns. There wasn't enough time. He knew she was in there. She wouldn't let her maw worry like this. If Kat were okay, she would be checking on everyone else.

Ian took off his t-shirt and wrapped it like a bandana around his nose and mouth and then sprinted toward the front door.

"Ian!" Mr. Cullen shouted behind him. "No! Wait for the truck."

Ian ducked inside the door, keeping low to the ground.

The fog of smoke immediately assailed him and he coughed. He couldn't see anything. He moved forward until he bumped into something. A railing. It came off in his hand. He crawled on hands and knees to the kitchen. He soaked his t-shirt with water and put it back around his nose and mouth and then made his way back to the stairs. He'd have to find his way to the second floor. She had to be there, trapped somewhere.

One. Step. At. A. Time. His knee stuck in a hole and he pulled out. His hand slipped off one side where the rail gave way. He counted each step to keep his bearings. One step. Two. Three. Four.

Finally he was on the landing.

He crawled to the right and listened at the door. Nothing. He pounded.

"Kat! Are you in there? Kat?"

Was that a scratching? Or his imagination.

He felt his way up to the doorknob. It was stuck. It wouldn't turn. The solid wooden door was too heavy for him to break down.

"Kat! If you can hear me, push on the door. It's stuck."

Again he only heard a small scratching sound, like a kitten was asking to come out.

He wrapped his hands around the knob and pulled with all he had. Nothing.

Ian took a part of the broken railing and pounded on the door near the frame, hoping to dislodge it even a little.

Again, he grabbed the knob and with all his strength yelled at the top of his lungs as he pulled. It opened and he fell backward coughing.

Crawling again he found Kat had fallen in the doorway. Her finger tapped almost silently on the floor.

Ian unwrapped the t-shirt from around his own mouth and tied it around hers. "Breathe," He told her. "I've got you."

He put his arms under her armpits and pulled her along with him as he crawled and scooted back to the stairs. Again, he counted the stairs as he moved back down them, one at a time. First he moved down a stair and then he scooted her down the stair. Him. Then her. Him. Then her.

Sometimes she would moan as her body hit one stair and then the next. He couldn't help it. He couldn't carry her without falling.

When he finally got to the last stair, two firemen were there to help. One took Kat in his arms. Ian collapsed. His energy spent.

IAN WOKE IN THE HOSPITAL. Mr. Cullen sat next to him legs stretched out as he leaned back in a chair.

"You're awake." He leaned forward to pat Ian's arm, and smiled.

Ian tried to sit up but started coughing. "Kat?" He eeked out her name.

"She's fine. You saved her, you know. I don't think the firemen would have found her in time. She's recovering in another room."

"Where?" he coughed again. "Want to… see her."

Mr. Cullen pushed him back against the pillow. "Take it easy. Don't do too much. She's fine, thanks to you. Her mother's with her, has been the last two days. If you hadn't given her your soaked t-shirt it might have been too much. We might have lost her."

Ian relaxed against the pillow.

"Is it my fault? Did I forget something? The bonfire? The fireplace?"

"No. Nothing like that. It was no one's fault." Mr. Cullen paused. "It was an electrical fire. Old wiring."

"The house?" Ian whispered.

"Gone. All of it." Mr. Cullen looked to the ceiling. "Nothing salvageable."

"Nothing?"

Mr. Cullen didn't speak.

Ian didn't know what to say. It was one thing to be kicked out of a house he never liked. But Mr. Cullen had raised his family there. Had nursed his wife and buried her there. He couldn't imagine what that must feel like.

Ian looked at the ceiling too. They were both screwed.

"Ian, I want you to know that no matter what happens you have a home with me. I don't want you to worry about where to live."

"Thanks Mr. Cullen but it looks like neither of us have a home now."

"Something will work out," Mr. Cullen said. "You just rest. You concentrate on getting better. Let me worry about where we will live."

CHAPTER 7

Gavin looked out to the Firth of Clyde one last time. Then he turned back to look up the hill where his home and Inn had been. It hadn't taken long to level the burned hulk and cart it away. The village had helped. Instead of spending their holiday relaxing as planned, they'd all shown up with shovels and dump trucks. They laid out food for everyone who worked that day. They brought extra clothing too.

When Theresa had offered for him and Ian to come to Oregon and stay with her on Mt. Hood, he was surprised. She didn't seem to be the same frightened and cautious woman he'd met that first day when Ian showed up. Then she was a woman who believed the world was a dark place and no one was to be trusted—particularly men.

Of course, Ian saving her daughter's life might have put a little kink in her outlook. But certainly not enough to wholeheartedly invite two strangers to America to share her home. Not that there was a romance or anything. She was just being kind. She said the climate in Oregon was very similar to Dunoon. He wondered.

Ian yelled from the car. "Everyone is ready, Mr. Cullen. Are you ready?"

Gavin waved and held up a finger to show he needed another minute.

The car door closed and he turned back to the hill once more. He remembered when he and Evelyn had first bought the old house in that summer more than twenty years ago. Rachel had been six and just starting school in the village. The sky had been clear blue, the air offering them new life and so many plans. They had blindly taken on the task of making it into a B&B, welcoming visitors from around the world. They had raised Rachel together. And they had said their goodbyes in that house.

He looked at the empty space again where the house once stood. He realized he had been standing still the last eight years since Evelyn's death. Rooted to their room together. Rooted to their life together. Not looking forward or backward, simply standing still, moving through each day in a fog. It wasn't until Rachel returned with her family and her friends that he realized he hadn't been living, he'd merely existed.

"Evelyn," he said as he looked toward the hill where she was buried. "I'm awake again. I don't know exactly where I'm going or what is to come. But I am free now. Thank you for loving me. I hope that one day I can pass it on."

He turned away and walked to the waiting car not looking back again. From now on he would only move forward.

It was a new day. A new year. A new life.

AFTERWORD

These stories feature the entire Sweetwater Canyon band and their families. If you liked this set of novellas and novelettes, I invite you to start at the beginning of the series. In fact, you can get the first novel for free by signing up to my email list. Click the picture to go directly to the sign up page.

Balancing a career and a relationship is never easy, and it's even harder when you are on the road and everyone wants a piece of you.

As a music major who sacrificed everything to become master of the upright bass, the last thing Michele Scott thought she'd be doing is touring with an Americana and Bluegrass band. But to tell the truth, she loves it.

Not so much David Blackstone. Even though he's irresistible, the thought of balancing her career, life on the road, and a long-distance relationship isn't for her. Her music gives her life, yet her heart yearns for something more. A girl just can't have it all… or can she? Trusting David is a risk that may give her everything she wants or it will close her heart forever.

GET YOUR FREE COPY NOW!

ABOUT THE AUTHOR

Maggie Lynch is the author of 20+ published books, as well as numerous short stories and non-fiction articles. Her fiction tells stories of men and women making heroic choices one messy moment at a time. Maggie is also the founder of Windtree Press, an independent publishing cooperative with over 150 titles among 20 authors.

Her love of lifelong-learning has garnered degrees in psychology, counseling, computer science, and education; and led to opportunities to consult in Europe, Australia, and the Middle East. Since 2013, Maggie and her musician husband have settled in the beautiful Pacific Northwest where she now enjoys the luxury of writing full-time.

For more information:
maggielynch.com
maggie@maggielynch.com

www.ingramcontent.com/pod-product-compliance
Lightning Source LLC
Chambersburg PA
CBHW032004180726
48283CB00008B/2564